PRAISE FOR

Black Brother, Black Brother

"Based on Dr. Jewell Parker Rhodes's own family experience, this **memorable, insightful story** about identity, family, revenge, and fencing **will delight and educate middle graders** and their parents."
—*GOOD MORNING AMERICA*

"**Inspiring and eye-opening**.... The **perfect read** for young readers." —*SHE READS*

"Another **unforgettable** book by **an author that is quickly becoming one of the most important creators of our time**." —*Colby Sharp, cofounder of NERDY BOOK CLUB*

★ "A **profound treatise** about institutional racism.... A **powerful work and must-have** for children's collections." —*BOOKLIST, starred review*

★ "A **moving** look at systemic racism and the school-to-prison pipeline. This **exhilarating and emotional** story shows young readers the power in fighting for what you believe and surrounding yourself with people who will fight with you."
—*BOOKPAGE, starred review*

★ "An **excellent** selection for both elementary and middle library collections, this is **a title that celebrates finding one's place in the world**."
—*SCHOOL LIBRARY CONNECTION, starred review*

"A **deeply critical insight for young readers**. Placing biracial boyhood and the struggles of colorism at its center, the novel **challenges readers to pursue their own self-definition**." —*KIRKUS REVIEWS*

"This novel offers **a solid story, with relatable, three-dimensional characters** considering identity, that will teach readers about colorism's effects." —*PUBLISHERS WEEKLY*

"Donte's story is **a good primer for younger readers on microaggressions**.... **Interesting and exciting**.... Give to readers who love Jason Reynolds's 'Track' series or Jewell Parker Rhodes's other offerings for young readers." —*SCHOOL LIBRARY JOURNAL*

"**A classic sports story**.... Readers who mourn the completion of Jason Reynolds' Track series will be happy to find Rhodes' take on revenge and redemption." —*THE BULLETIN*

BLACK BROTHER, BLACK BROTHER

Jewell Parker Rhodes

LITTLE, BROWN AND COMPANY

New York Boston

YA
RHO
CAUDZLL
2023

Little, Brown and Company
Hachette Book Group
1290 Avenue of the Americas, New York, NY 10104
Visit us at LBYR.com

Originally published in hardcover and ebook by Little, Brown and Company in March 2020
First Trade Paperback Edition: March 2021

Little, Brown and Company is a division of Hachette Book Group, Inc.
The Little, Brown name and logo are trademarks of
Hachette Book Group, Inc.

The Library of Congress has cataloged the hardcover edition as follows:
Names: Rhodes, Jewell Parker, author.
Title: Black brother, black brother / by Jewell Parker Rhodes.
Description: New York : Little, Brown and Company, [2020] | Audience: Ages 8–12. | Summary: Suspended unjustly from elite Middlefield Prep, Donte Ellison studies fencing with a former champion, hoping to put the racist fencing team captain in his place.
Identifiers: LCCN 2019034929 | ISBN 9780316493802 (hardcover) | ISBN 9780316493819 (ebook) | ISBN 9780316428934
Subjects: CYAC: Fencing—Fiction. | African Americans—Fiction. | Racism—Fiction. | Preparatory schools—Fiction. | Schools—Fiction. | Family life—Massachusetts—Fiction. | Massachusetts—Fiction.
Classification: LCC PZ7.R3476235 Bl 2020 | DDC [Fic]—dc23
LC record available at https://lccn.loc.gov/2019034929

ISBNs: 978-0-316-49379-6 (pbk.), 978-0-316-49381-9 (ebook)

Printed in the United States of America

LSC-H

Printing 4, 2021

Dedicated to
Phillip Mackert
a special reader

1
THE CRIME

BLACK BOY

I wish I were invisible. Wearing Harry Potter's Invisibility Cloak or Frodo Baggins's Elvish ring. Whether shrouded in fabric or slipping on gold, it wouldn't matter to me. I'd be gone. Disappeared.

I stare at my hands. Nighttime dark. They have a life of their own. Clenching, unclenching. Fist then no fist. I keep my shoulders relaxed; my face, bland. My hands won't behave.

No science fiction or fantasy is going to help me. I live in a too-real world.

Sitting, I stare at the black specks on the white linoleum. A metaphor? That's what they're teaching me in English. *Metaphor.* Except I won't believe I'm just a black speck. I'm bigger, more than that. Though sometimes I feel like I'm swimming in whiteness.

Most of the students at Middlefield Prep don't look like me.

They don't like me either.

I look up. The secretary, Mrs. Kay, even the assistant headmaster, Mr. Waters, with his tartan tie, avert their eyes. They've been staring, wondering:

How come he gets in so much trouble? Why can't he be good like his brother? Helpful? Obedient.

Under my breath, I curse. My stomach twists.

Be invisible.

My insides burn. Anger builds. This has nothing to do with me.

I'm not here. Donte is not here.

My right foot taps uncontrollably. If I sit any longer, I'll explode.

"Donte," Headmaster McGeary says warily.

I stand. "Sir." (Be cool, I tell myself.)

"It's 2:46 PM. Couldn't you have finished the day without getting in trouble?"

This isn't the way it's supposed to go down. He's supposed to call me into his office. Shut the door, talk privately with me.

Now he's scolding me in public.

The headmaster's eyelids are heavy, puffy. He's tired, but I'm tired, too. Every week, I'm punished for something I didn't do.

I clutch my left fist with my hand. It's still trying to move, open and shut. My right leg trembles.

Mr. Waters smirks; the secretary's eyes show pity. Pity pushes me over the edge.

"I didn't do anything," I blurt. "Like the time before, and the time before that. And the time before that. I didn't do anything."

The two men grow taller, rigid. Bracing, readying to take me down. They don't like me too loud.

I exhale. My dad's been to war. Two tours. No matter what I do, I'm outflanked.

I quiet my voice, try to speak reasonably.

In my head, I hear: *Speak truth to power.* Mom's favorite phrase. Then, Dad adding, *Respectfully.*

I try to still my body. But I feel a trembling in my hands, up my spine.

The wall clock's minute hand clicks. 2:48 PM.

"I hate this school," I say softly, slowly, trying to make them understand.

"Hate no matter what goes wrong, I'm at fault. Some guy overturns a chair; it's my fault. My locker's broken into; my supplies scattered, dumped in the trash. My books ripped. I get detention. *And* a library fine."

My voice races, rises.

"In gym, playing ball, I get called for fouls all the time. But nobody is called when I'm fouled."

My hands clench, unclench.

"Everybody here bullies me. Teachers. Students. Whispers, sometimes outright shouts follow me. Seems like everybody has something bad to say: 'You dress thug.' 'Your dreads are dreadful.' Girls laugh and point at me. 'Why can't you be like your brother?'

6

'Can your brother find you in the dark?'" I breathe. "It hurts. All of it."

I stop. My stomach churns.

Three faces. Mr. Waters is grim. Mrs. Kay, embarrassed by my outburst, looks down, pulling her ear.

The headmaster's cheeks flush, his eyes glare.

I've lit the fire. I need Harry's Invisibility Cloak. Need to disappear, escape this bright office with its stacked trophy case and laminated Massachusetts map with a stenciled #1 above two crossed swords.

Headmaster McGeary steps forward. "You don't get to bring your New York behavior here. You don't get to yell at me or anyone else."

"I didn't yell at you."

"Are you contradicting me?"

"No. Frustrated," I say, exasperated. "You didn't even ask me how I got here. I don't want to be here. I don't want to be in trouble."

"You *are* in trouble."

"Ask me what I did."

He frowns.

"Ask me what I did," I insist.

Nothing.

The clock clicks another minute. The office door opens. Dylan, a classmate, stops, looks, walks backward, then shuts the door. (Come back, I want to call.)

Nine minutes until school ends.

"I didn't do anything. Not ever. Not today."

"Seventh grade. Six more years at Middlefield. I suggest you learn to get along."

"I try to get along. Everyone's been against me since I started. Especially Alan. Today, he throws a pencil. It hits Samantha. I didn't throw it. Sam screams. Ms. Wilson turns from the whiteboard and looks at me. *Me.* Nobody else.

"And now I'm here. You don't even ask me what happened. You don't care. You don't." I slap angrily at my tears.

Mrs. Kay stands. Her eyes are kind. I think she might comfort me.

The headmaster waves her away, then sighs. "Why can't you be more like your brother?"

Fury, roiling spasms. It hurts to breathe. (Get control, I tell myself.)

I bend, trying to hide my pain. Quiet my hands.

"Your brother is a good boy."

(Keep it together.)

Five more minutes to go. Three o'clock. Not fair. Not fair. The words rattle in my head.

My backpack is on a chair. I pick it up.

I hate, hate this school. Hate our family moved. Hate how people treat me.

A murmur, then a roar: "I hate being me."

Disgusted, I swing my backpack. *Bam.* It slams at my feet.

"Call security," says Mr. Waters.

Mrs. Kay backs away. She's scared. Of me.

I cringe.

"No, the police," says Headmaster.

He's done with me.

The plan all along. Get me out of Middlefield Prep.

THE WALK

I'm not invisible. Worst time ever not to have a superpower.

School buses—not the yellow kind—are boarding. These buses are called "coaches." They even have Wi-Fi and TV screens built into the seats. Parents pick up kids in SUVs, Mercedes-Benzes, and Teslas. Some kids order Ubers, Lyfts. No bikes or skateboards here.

All students wear blue blazers with gold buttons. Each blazer has a badge with the initials *MP*, two swords making an *X*, and *Non Nobis Solum*.

Seeing me, flanked by cops, the crowd quiets.

Even though white plastic circles my wrists,

pulling my hands behind my back, tight, I keep my head high.

There are dozens of people. Might as well be hundreds. Folks are snapping pictures, recording videos. By evening, everyone will know the new kid—Donte Ellison—was arrested.

"Donte, Donte, what'd you do?"

I scowl.

"Get out of the way, kid," says the officer, his hand on my back, pushing me forward faster.

"He's my brother," answers Trey.

Bewildered, the officer stops, studies Trey. "You have a black brother?"

Quick, like lightning, Alan repeats, "Black brother, black brother."

I wince.

The officer opens the car door. My head is pushed down, and my body follows, collapsing, folding into the patrol car. The other officer gets behind the wheel.

"What'd you do?" Trey's yell penetrates the glass.

I turn from my brother's face. He should know I didn't do anything.

The second officer gets in the car. Steel mesh and

unbreakable glass separate the front seat from the back. I'm sitting on hard vinyl. There aren't any handles to unlock the back doors.

"I'm sorry. Donte. I'm sorry." My brother taps the window, trying to get me to look at him. "I know you didn't do anything. Didn't do a thing."

"Hey," shouts the cop, rolling down his window. "Son, you don't want to get involved in this."

Trey stops tapping. I look at him. Miserable, he stands, looking lost, on the curb.

Even if my hands were untied, there's no tab for me to lower the window. I could shout, "It's okay. It's okay." Though I'd be lying.

I don't want Trey to feel bad, but I *do* want him to feel bad. I keep quiet.

The car moves. Students swarm behind my brother. Some even run behind the police car as it slowly navigates past gawking people, parked and stopped cars, and limo coaches.

"Don't want to hurt anybody," the nondriving officer says.

12

Alan slaps the window.

"Get away, kid," the second officer shouts.

I turn away. Alan slaps the window again to make me look at him. (As if he knows no policeman will ever arrest him.)

"Hey. Black brother."

Trey dashes forward, shoving him away. But the damage is done.

Pumping a fist, Alan leads his fencing crew. "Black brother, black brother." Louder, then louder still. They jog on either side of the patrol car.

Head low, hands cuffed, I can't escape. Nowhere to hide.

Day one, Alan made school miserable for me. "King Alan," they call him. Captain of the fencing team. He says "black" like a slur. Says it real nasty. Like a worse word. A word he thinks but doesn't dare say.

When he met Trey, he laughed, pointing at me, mocking. "Black brother. Black brother."

My new nickname. The whole school seemed to whisper it. Or else thought it.

Funny, how with two words, Alan made it easier

for kids to exclude me. If I sat in the cafeteria, students moved. No one invited me to a study group. Or offered to be friends. No one even wanted to talk with me.

Alan, the cool kid, had drawn a line, and sucking up to him, everyone turned against me.

"Let's go," says the cop. The car picks up speed down the long, tree-lined driveway. Alan and his teammates can't keep pace. Some hunch, catching their breath. Others hold their sides.

I twist around, seeing the gossiping crowd, the swarm of cars, hearing, "Black brother, black brother... Black brother, black brother." (A warped singsong.)

Alan waves goodbye.

The headmaster stands beneath two flapping flags: the American Stars and Stripes and Middlefield Prep's blue-and-gold sword insignia. Trey stands on the grassy area that shapes the circular roundabout. He must be cold. Like me, he isn't wearing a coat. Arms crossed about his chest, blank-faced, he keeps staring at the departing car. Danny, Alan's lieutenant, taunts him. Shouts—*what?*—in Trey's ear.

Trey keeps watching. Trying to see my face in the car's rear window.

I turn, stare at the traffic, the back of the cops' heads.

Black brother, black brother...black brother, black brother. The patrol car is beyond school sight. Beyond sound. But the chant still chases me.

It starts to snow.

Crying, my chin touches my chest.

Black is not invisible.

JAIL

"**This is a** satellite station. Not as crowded as a regular jail. Adults have been grouped together. So, you've got your own cell.

"Safer," said the cop, turning the key.

Funny, I don't feel safe. (Unnerved, threatened.)

Across the narrow corridor, six men are watching me. Some are curious; some stare, blankly. Some black, some white. Two, hateful, glare at me.

I sit, my back toward the men, studying the concrete wall like the lines, cracks, and scratched curses are a complicated puzzle.

My right leg tremors, bouncing uncontrollably. I want to cry, Get me out of here. I feel like I'm suffocating. Fluorescent lights buzz overhead. There aren't any windows. Just an awful smell of bleach mixed with sweat and vomit.

My cell is small. A metal toilet is in the corner. It doesn't have a lid.

Across from me, men can see if I pee. Or worse. I'll never go to the bathroom here.

Sitting on the stone bench, I feel ashamed. Even though I didn't do anything wrong.

"What'd you do?" asks a gruff voice.

There it is. Guilty. Even Trey thought I was guilty.

"What'd you do?"

I don't want to answer.

I hear Dad: *Be respectful of adults.* Even if they're locked up?

But Dad's not here to ask.

"Nothing," I mutter without turning around. Then, I add, "Sir."

Nausea rises. I swallow, choking back the nasty taste.

I'm confused. A cloud settles over me. Making me more anxious and scared.

In New York, I had plenty friends. In Newton, everybody's suspicious of me.

New kid, new school, I get pushed around. I get that. I'm not as tall as Trey. Not as strong or athletic. None of it is Trey's fault. Not really. Yet I wish he was here instead of me. Wish he felt worse than me.

I'm not a good brother, I think.

I feel worthless.

Of all the kids in the school, the police found it easy to arrest me. Why was Mrs. Kay scared? Why did Mr. Waters seem to enjoy my troubles? Worse, why did Headmaster call the police on me? Since I've been at Middlefield, the police never came for anyone else.

Is something wrong with me?

Mom and Dad say I'm the best son ever. But they say that about Trey, too.

The cloud is getting bigger; it's darkening, filling up my spirit and cell. I don't understand. Last year, I liked being me.

Friends in New York liked me. They knew me forever. Teasing, playing, talking with me. But maybe they didn't have a choice? I was Trey's little brother. I was always around.

Everybody liked Trey.

Even at Middlefield Prep, they like Trey. Why not me?

I know why. Despair wells, my body aches.

"Hey, kid. Kid?" The voice is deep, almost soothing.

I won't look.

"You'll get used to it."

Jail. I tighten my throat, dash, collapse over the toilet, and throw up. I'm a kid. I'm not supposed to be here. I'm not supposed to be here. I cough. My stomach heaves again.

Men's laughter swirls, echoes in my cell.

Disappear. Be invisible.

Shame overwhelms me.

RESCUE:
IN BLACK & WHITE

Mom rescues me. In my cell, I hear her fierce lawyer-talk, demanding my release. Minutes later, a red-haired policeman opens my cell, guiding me, not gently, into the lobby.

Mom holds me; I hold tight, too. I smell her fear. Her fear makes me more afraid.

Over Mom's shoulder, I see Dad walk in. "Where's my son?" Dad's big. Six feet four. Not heavy. Solid, strong. He wraps his arms around me and Mom.

For seconds, I feel safe. Feel the world is right again.

The cop clears his throat. A sergeant behind the desk straightens. They smile slightly at Dad. They never smiled at Mom.

Trying to be pleasant, they give Dad forms to sign. Say I'm in his care until my hearing.

Dad doesn't speak.

The cop stares at Dad's signature. Connects his last name to mine.

"Sure it's all a misunderstanding," says the red-haired cop, almost jovial. "Boys will be boys."

Dad towers over him, his gaze harsh. Mom holds my hand, watching the two men. Mom is short. I'm even taller than her.

"I'm Officer Williams. In charge of community policing. We work hard to keep our community safe."

("Then why arrest me?" I nearly shout.) Mom pulls me close.

The officer extends his hand as if he and Dad could be friends.

Dad, who always talks about respect, glares. Doesn't shake his hand.

Mom's mouth presses into a thin, tight line.

Dad guides Mom and me outside.

Weird. Mom's the lawyer. Yet, for the police, it was Dad who seemed to matter most.

HOME

Mom can't stop talking. She does that when she's angry or scared. Tonight, she's both. Plus, she's a lawyer and talks a lot anyway. Now she's in overdrive.

"School-to-prison pipeline. This is how it starts. Arresting kids of color. How come they didn't call us? Why didn't the principal call?"

Mom is fierce. Dad drives the car. It's winter, early darkness blurs shapes, inside and outside the car. My face is hidden. And I'm glad. Dad's face is lit by the dashboard's glow.

"Police before parents. Unbelievable."

"Aren't you going to ask me what I did?"

Mom twists in her seat. She clasps my freed hands. "Donte, I don't need to ask. I know you. Nothing you did could justify you being handcuffed."

I can hear the wail hiding in her voice. In the rearview mirror, Dad looks back at me.

Funny, Mom looks out for me. Dad and me look out for her.

"I'm okay, Mom."

She exhales. "This is how it starts. Bias. Racism. Plain and simple. Philadelphia, cops called on black men meeting in Starbucks. Portland, cops called on a hotel guest talking on his cell phone with his mother.

"That's not the worst of it. Cleveland, Tamir Rice playing with a toy gun, killed. Twelve and he's dead.

"Boys. Men. It's everywhere. Everywhere." Panic, grief.

(I wish Mom would stop talking. Everything she says, I know. But her saying it out loud makes me feel worse.)

The garage door opens.

Mom whimpers. Dad leans, kisses her. I reach over the back seat, touching her hair.

We all get out of the car. The overhead garage light casts a dull glow. To the left are stacked boxes labeled with a felt marker: **Xmas Ornaments**; several boxes with a big **B** for books. But the majority of boxes are marked either **Trey's Treasures** or **Donte's Treasures**. Inside these boxes are every sports certificate, every assignment, every art project Trey and me ever did. Mom saves it all.

I wonder if Mom will save a keepsake from the day I went to jail? That's not fair. My anger mixes with my shame. I love Mom more than anything.

Mom shakes herself. She wipes her cheeks. "Donte, I'm going to cook for you."

Dad and me exchange glances. Mom hates cooking. She hugs me. "I love you, Donte. I love you, I love you. We're going to fight this." She's Lioness Mom again.

"Dad?" I ask, my voice cracking, after Mom leaves. (I'm trying to ask without asking: Did I do all right?

But what's *right* in jail?)

Dad squeezes my shoulder. "I'm proud of you. I know it was hard."

I bury my face against Dad's chest. He holds me, steady as a rock.

"What's it mean 'Every day above ground is a good day'?"

"Who said that?"

"A man in the cell across from me. Said, 'Black folks, every day above ground is a good day.' He sounded sad."

Dad says fiercely, "For everybody, living above ground is a good day." But his sagging shoulders give him away. He knows I'm more vulnerable than him.

"Don't tell Mom." His hands spasm, clenching, unclenching.

I can't help grinning. Dad and me are alike. Feelings ripple through our muscles and bones.

Dad would never hurt anyone; neither would I. But we have this furnace inside and it gets hot, physical.

Dad's grandparents were Norwegian. Maybe Viking ancestry makes us explode? Dad looks the part. A Viking king.

Compared to him, I'm a shrimp.

Dad's eyes are blue; mine, brown. His hair falls in long blond waves; my hair twists in black dreads. I take after Mom's side of the family. Short, compact. White skin, brown skin. Mom's family is descended from captured Africans. Dad's family were poor seafarers from Norway.

"Your mother's right," says Dad. "It's racism, pure and simple. No, not pure, not simple. Ugly. Diseased.

"We'll beat it."

Dad's words soothe me. Still, I feel doubt. I was *there*. He wasn't. I was the one cuffed, isolated in the back seat, driven to jail.

I shiver, remembering my cell.

Newspapers, television, books, and movies always show the bad guy caught.

Maybe something's wrong with me?

Everyone in school thinks so. Headmasters, teachers. Even Trey doubted me.

"Donte, I love you. Don't forget that." Dad's gaze makes me feel warm like goodness bathing me.

"I know." And I do know. "Love you, too."

Dad hugs me, giving me a hard pat on the back. The pat tells me Dad knows I'm strong.

In my old neighborhood, my friends were multiracial. Middlefield Prep makes me feel alien. In my old school, basketball ruled. Trey was "top dog." At Middlefield Prep, fencing is the be-all. Nobody fences better than Alan.

I shiver. Never thought there'd be a time when Mom and Dad couldn't protect me. Is this growing up? (Does Trey feel this, too?)

"Let's go inside. See what your mom is cooking. Probably scrambled eggs."

As I follow Dad, my smile drips, slides away. The cloud from the jail has followed me home. Don't want to upset Mom and Dad any further. (Pretend cool, I think.)

Yet, my spirit knows...going to court isn't going to make it any better.

Middlefield College Preparatory School
v. Donte Roman Ellison

Despite Mom's skill, despite what she and Dad believe,
I don't think I'm going to win.

I feel like I'm going to lose.

I'm lost.

SUSPENDED

Trey thinks a week of suspension is a vacation. It isn't.

I'm out of step with the world. Nowhere to go. Nothing to do.

Mom works at the Legal Aid Society. "I seek justice for everybody," she says. Lawyering for social justice.

Dad is a computer architect. He designs computer systems for big companies. He likes being a geek, and when he isn't working, he plays *Warcraft*.

Trey goes to school. Even though he says he hates it, he doesn't. He has no trouble making friends. He's good at every sport. Except he's never fenced. He's a rising star on the basketball team. Soccer, too.

We moved. Mom said she was needed in Massachusetts. I believe that. (For real.)

Mom works in Boston. Maybe it's better there? But we live in Newton. A suburb.

Our neighborhood is rich, which means it's mainly—I mean, *really, really*—all white. "Good schools," Mom says. Which means its private schools are even better than public schools. Middlefield Prep is supposed to be the best.

Mom says, "Being well educated is the best way to fight prejudice."

Now I wonder. If I'm smart enough for Middlefield Prep (and I am) how come they still suspended me and had me jailed?

On TV, there was a video loop of a school officer pulling a girl from her desk, slamming, dragging her across the floor. Stuff like that isn't supposed to happen at rich schools. (Though it shouldn't be happening anywhere.)

How come schools with black and brown kids are

mostly poor? How come they never seem to be the best—or even good?

It isn't fair.

I'm riled again. Need to move. Get out. Even inside my house, I feel imprisoned.

I slip my down jacket over my hoodie. If Mom were here, she'd say, "Take off your hoodie. People might think you're a thug."

Middlefield thinks I'm a thug even when I'm wearing my school uniform. The uniform is supposed to make us all the same. A blue blazer doesn't mean we're treated equal.

So, what's the point?

I unlock the front door. The air is brisk. My inside self is so hot, the cold on my face feels good.

Snowflakes swirl. I stuff my hands in my pockets and start walking.

Newton *is* beautiful. Big brick homes with white-painted shutters. Smoke swirling out of chimney stacks. Even barren oak trees flanking both sides of the street make it seem postcard-ready. Light snow on the road, on tree limbs, adds magic. I get it—who wouldn't want to live here?

Except me. Me, I've got to be careful.

Behind curtains is someone wondering:

Why isn't he in school? Why's he here? In our neighborhood?

What if someone didn't get the message that the Ellison family had integrated the neighborhood? That they have two biracial sons? Actually, multiracial. I'm Scotch-Irish, Norwegian, and African (Mom thinks Nigerian and Congolese).

I slow. Nikes keep me from slipping, but I still feel like I'm falling.

I start shivering, trembling all at once. Shivering because of the cold, trembling because of my mixed-up feelings.

Black brother, black brother. I turn, thinking someone is taunting me.

The street is quiet. Not even a person. Or a person walking a dog.

I face forward.

Black brother, black brother.

Black brother is all Middlefield Prep can see.

Then there's *me*. Skin color is just a part of me.

I squat, right on the sidewalk, feeling crazy, overcome. It hurts to think for Alan, a kid like me, my inside self, doesn't matter.

I panic. I've got to stand. Someone might call the police.

Black brother. Words are being carried by the wind. No one else but me can hear it. My mind is blown.

Alan wanted other students to see only my blackness. See it as a stain.

I remember Alan's contorted, electrified face yelling at me outside the police car.

Like I conjured it, a squad car turns the corner. Turning too fast toward home, I slip. My gloved hand lands on ice.

I stagger up.

The patrol car slows. My heart races. Two officers stare. I push my hood away from my face. Let them see me. Let them know I've nothing to hide.

Sirens blare. I freeze. Red and blue lights flash. My heart beats fierce.

I want to run. Faster than I've ever run before. But something horrible might happen.

Exhaling, I close my eyes, waiting to be arrested.

The siren's wail becomes more distant. Amazingly, the black and white speeds down the street.

Crime must be elsewhere. Or maybe not?

Maybe it's another black kid walking on the street, on the road? Just walking?

Trying to mind his own business.

Like me.

I stop, listening to the wind, the red bird chirping in the tree. Everyone is off to work, or school, or inside their homes staying warm.

But not me. (It's not fair.)

Smoke twirls from brick chimneys. Not far off from this quiet space is a whole world, a suburb, Middlefield Prep.

I can't prove myself to the whole world. But I can take on Alan. Stop his disrespect.

Show him he won't defeat me.

He's not better than me.

MAKING PLANS

Soon as I hear the door opening, I run to the hall. "Trey, I've been waiting for you."

"Thought you were mad at me."

"Naw. Not mad—" I press my lips. "Okay, I was mad. But I'm not mad anymore. I need your help."

Trey's eyebrows arch just like Dad's. He stands tall. A foot taller than me. His gym bag swings from his arm, stinking up the hall.

"I let you down." Trey's face droops. "I'm sorry. I should've known you were innocent."

I don't want to go back to that moment. To that

hurt. "It's okay," I say. Then, whisper fiercely, "I want to beat Alan. Make him take it back."

Trey high-fives me. "That's what I'm talking about. Glue in his jockstrap. Flood his locker. Dump his fencing gear in the pool. Can you imagine? See his face?" Trey grins, rubs his hands together. "King Alan embarrassed."

"No, not just embarrassed," I say, serious, my voice still low. "Humiliated. Like he humiliated me."

Trey's face stills. "Mom and Dad won't like this."

"Yeah, I know." I keep whispering, even though Mom and Dad aren't home. I know I should "turn the other cheek," "be stronger," "be the better man."

"Payback." Trey could always tell what I was thinking.

"Yeah, payback. For real."

Trey drops his bag, moving toward the kitchen. "I need something to eat."

I can't help but smile. Trey grows like a giant. After practice, he drinks a half gallon of milk. Chews three ham sandwiches. But when he's worried, he eats even more.

In the kitchen, I start slathering whole wheat bread with mayonnaise. "Wish I could sue Alan. Sue all prejudiced people. Because what Alan thinks, he makes other people think, too. So, I'm suspended. Going before a judge. Middlefield says I'm a delinquent."

"Mom's going to fix it," says Trey, too quickly. (I can tell he's as worried as me.)

"It isn't fair." My fist clenches. I'm heated, losing control. "Zero tolerance," I rage.

"Means harsh punishment for almost anything," Mom explained. "Talking back in school. Carrying a cell phone. Refusing to go to the office."

Slamming a backpack.

(A snowball going back to Alan.)

"He should feel what he makes me feel," I shout. (Small. Hated.)

I smash the sandwich. Mayonnaise oozes.

Trey's smart. People-smart. He knows I'm about to cry. "There's nothing wrong with you." Trey stares steadily at me.

I lower my eyes first. I hate how Alan—the whole school—makes me doubt me.

Trey grabs another slice of bread. "Maybe I should put some lettuce on this?" He looks at me. Then shakes his head. "Naw."

"Tomatoes?"

"Nope, extra mayo." He dips the knife into the jar. "Mayo is a vegetable, right?"

Feeling better, I smile. Trey, like Dad, can say, do something offbeat and lighten heaviness, sadness.

Mouth full, Trey mumbles, "Only thing Alan really cares about is fencing."

"Captain of the state championship team."

"That's right." He gulps milk from the carton. "It's his whole life."

My life's upside down—why not Alan's? What if *he* loses rather than wins?

"You could take him, Trey. Bet you could."

"Not my fight." Trey takes another bite.

"You're good at sports. Great, even. Try."

"Really? Win your battle?" Trey's blue eyes, so like Dad's, study me. "You know what Dad would say."

"Yeah, 'personal responsibility.'" My heel *tap-taps*.

40

My arms shudder; hands, clench. I'm back in the head-master's office, back in jail.

Trey licks mayo from his fingers, chomps on the last piece of bread.

"Then I'll learn fencing."

Trey chokes. "What?"

"I'll learn fencing."

He belly-laughs.

"Don't laugh," I shout.

"You and sports? You don't like sports."

"I'll learn."

"Coordination, speed, agility. You need them for sports. PlayStation doesn't count."

I shove Trey. Rebalancing, his hand swipes and the milk falls to the floor.

Trey shoves back.

I clutch his waist. He pushes back, clasps me around my back. We wrestle. Our shoes slip. Trey's long leg sweeps behind my knee. I fall. My shirt soaks up milk.

Trey straddles me. "Uncle."

Trey always beats me wrestling. I relax, making him think I'm giving up. With strength I didn't know

I had, I flip Trey. My knees are on either side of him, pinning him.

"Hey." Trey arches. My body presses him down.

"Uncle," says Trey.

But I don't let him up.

"Uncle."

I don't let go.

Grunting, Trey lifts up, grips, and turns me over like I'm a sack of potatoes. "Donte, it's going to be okay."

"No, it won't." Defeated, I sit cross-legged, not caring about the spilled milk.

Trey throws his hand over my shoulder. "Baby brother. Baby brother."

I won't look at him. (When Trey was five, I was three, Mom says Trey loved calling, "Baby Brother.")

Trey sighs. "Problem is you don't have any game."

"Help me get some." How could I explain that even if it were impossible to defeat Alan, I wanted to try?

"I've never known anybody who fenced. Except for Middlefield students. People like Alan."

"You mean rich? We're rich enough for private school."

"Tuition isn't like giving millions for the gymnasium. That's why it's called Alan Davies Family Gymnasium. Alan, Middlefield's Alan, is Alan Davies the Fourth."

"You kidding me?"

"Wish I was. You'll never beat Alan at his own game." Trey squeezes my shoulder, stands. "I'm going to shower, change my clothes."

I feel hopeless. Trapped all over again. I try to stand and slip. My knee cracks on the linoleum. I won't cry out. Won't complain. I can't beat the whole world, but I can beat Alan. I know I can. Just got to find another way.

I unspool the paper towels. Soak up the milk. (Be cool.

I'll find a way.)

I walk gingerly toward my room, hoping my pants won't drip on the carpet. The only good thing about the move is that Trey and me don't have to share a bedroom. We share a bathroom with connecting doors.

I see Trey peering at his chin in the long mirror. He

wishes he could shave. Dad didn't grow a beard until college. Still, Trey hopes. His hair wet is dark brown. Once it's dry, it'll billow in blond waves. Shirtless, I see how strong he is. Muscles in his shoulders, arms, and stomach. He's the athlete. Not me.

Trey's head turns.

(He knows what I'm thinking.)

He shrugs, helplessly.

Trey's skin is like Dad's; mine is like Mom's.

Brothers.

Students at Middlefield Prep think we're funny. "How can you be brothers?"

But it's Alan who punishes, who makes me being darker than my brother a crime.

Despairing, I gently close my bedroom door.

REVELATION

My comforter covers my head. I pretend-sleep. No more dinner table chatter. Or Mom smiling way too bright. Or Dad telling dumb Monty Python jokes.

No need to fake a smile. No need to avoid looking at Trey, swirling peas and carrots on the plate.

Alone, cocooned, I pretend there's no hurt in the outside world.

When I was younger, Mom and Dad always tucked me in. Since middle school, they haven't. But tonight, I hear my bedroom door opening.

"Donte," Mom calls softly, and I hear her yearning. She wants me happy. "Donte."

Dad edges closer and stands still above my bed.

(I'm not here.) He reaches out, patting the comforter. Though I can't feel his hand, I know he's loving me.

When we were kids, Mom told Trey and me about *Loving v. Virginia*. A black woman and a white man were sentenced to a year in prison for marrying each other. In 1967, the Supreme Court said state bans on interracial marriage violated the Equal Protection Clause of the Fourteenth Amendment to the US Constitution.

(Nineteen sixty-seven!!!!)

"Who knew," Mom says, her voice filling with amazement, "that an inner-city Pennsylvania girl would meet a rural, upstate New York boy and discover true love?"

"I knew you were the one at once," says Dad. "First glance."

Kiss, kiss, hug. Little, Trey and me always giggled, groaned. But we didn't really mind. We knew Mom and Dad loved...still love...each other so much.

Did they ever imagine having two sons?

White brother? Black brother?

I bury my mouth in the pillow. (Mom, Dad, please, go away.) I focus, keeping my breath calm, even though I want to rage.

Mom and Dad tiptoe out. Close the door.

I push away the comforter, stare at the wall. It reminds me of my cell.

Tomorrow, another suspension day.

"Donte? Donte?" The connecting bathroom door opens. Light shines and makes me squint. "Donte?"

Trey is a dark shadow. Light glows about him like a halo.

"Hey."

Trey offers a magazine article. I don't reach for it. I'm still upset.

Trey sets it down on the comforter right above my stomach. "Ellison brothers stick together," he says, extending his hand.

Like a lifeline, I clasp his hand. (Black against

white.) Then, we bump knuckles, clasp hands again. Trey's fist taps over his heart. I tap my heart, too.

"Brothers."

I don't know who says it first. Maybe our words overlap? Or we speak at the same time? I only know it's good to hear us say it:

"Brothers."

I reach for Trey's hand.

All night, I study the grainy photo. A black man dressed in fencing-suit white. Stretch pants, white socks, and shoes. Long-sleeved shirt and a high-neck vest overlay. One hand holds a mask. The other hand is gloved, holding a sword diagonally across his chest.

UNKNOWN BOSTON GREATS

Arden Jones is an African American foil fencer who won individual silver at the national championship, but wasn't able to lead the USA team to glory at the International Grand Prix. He competed but didn't score on the 1976 Olympic team. His teammate Peter Westbrook became the first African American to medal (bronze) in Olympic sabre.

Mr. Jones serves as facilities manager for the Boston Boys and Girls Club.

The article is dated April 22, 2019.

Arden Jones must still be alive. Still working at the Boys and Girls Club.

I trace Arden Jones's face. He's glaring at the camera. Tough. As if to say to the photographer, the whole world, "You can't touch me."

Yeah, I think. I want to be him. Arden Jones.

At the bottom of the page, Trey scrawled an address.

Then:

P.S. July—Fencing Team Tryouts

Way to go, big brother.

Snap.

King Alan, dethroned.

QUEST

"Ellison brothers are the greatest," Trey yells, heading off to school.

Dad says, "Watch *Black Panther*. Make some cocoa. It's cold outside."

Mom says, "Study algebra." Most schools teach Algebra Two in high school. Middlefield Prep accelerates everything. But it's cool, I'm good at it.

"Yeah. Sure. Sure. Bye," I say.

I wait ten minutes to make sure no one doubles back. No one has forgotten anything.

From my back pocket, I unfold the article. Arden Jones is who I need. He's going to teach. Help me make the Middlefield Prep fencing team.

My hero.

Donte Ellison, Fencer *Extraordinaire*.

TRY AND TRY AGAIN

The Boys and Girls Club is nearly empty. No kids. They're still in school. Some grown-ups are playing checkers at the desk. A woman with long, red-painted nails taps a keyboard. No one pays me any attention.

I search for Arden Jones.

The club is old-fashioned, in need of repair. Wall paint is cracked, peeling. The floors need sanding, varnishing. Dusty windows block the outdoor sun.

Veering left, I discover the gym. The basketball court isn't regulation size like Middlefield Prep's. And instead of a net, they just have a metal hoop for balls to pass through. Wood bleachers rather than steel flank the court. I peek into a side room. The weight room only has free weights. No circuit training, ellipticals, or treadmills. Pretty bare-bones. Makes me wonder why city kids can't have a rec center better than a hundred middle and high school students at Middlefield Prep? Even the locker room is pathetic. Open shelves. Two showers. Three toilets. Not enough facilities for a team.

Wandering, nobody bothering me, I search for Mr. Jones.

A man in a khaki uniform digs in a storage closet. He bounces out basketballs, dodgeballs, and rubber balls. Then he drags traffic cones onto the court, spacing them a foot apart. Dribble challenges, I think. Trey's good at them.

I walk across the gym, eager for a fencing teacher. I watch and wait.

"Can I help you?"

"Looking for Arden Jones."

"That's me."

I gasp, knowing I'm rude. But this isn't Arden Jones. He seems beat, weathered. Everything about him is gray. Gray beard. Gray hair and an ashy pallor. He's wrinkled; his legs, skeleton-thin.

This isn't Arden Jones daring the world. Standing triumphant.

"Can I help you?"

I turn, walking away, stunned that Arden Jones is an old man. Stunned that he's not the athlete I expected. Stunned, he seems defeated. An Olympian, here? In the Boys and Girls Club?

Mostly, I feel ashamed, disbelieving that I even thought he could help me.

Trey tried to help, but I wish I'd never seen the bio and photo of the strong young man. That Arden Jones is gone, disappeared.

"Why aren't you in school?"

"You think I'm a dropout."

"Are you?"

"A poor, inner-city kid?"

"Nothing wrong with that."

I stop. "You're right."

Mom says, "Money doesn't alter human rights, common equality." Then why do I let Alan's taunts make me feel small, less than?

(Is it because he's white with money? Or just white? Or because I'm black and, to him, a target?)

"You okay, son?"

Mr. Jones's eyes pierce me, sharp like a blade. I feel like he's sized me up. Seen my flaws, vulnerabilities.

His body seems loose, calm. But his right palm contracts—not into a fist, into a grip like he's holding a sword. Lean, strong, his fingers flex. His hand doesn't lie.

Suddenly I sense the young man he (once) was. His gaze and movements, aggressive, fierce. Him seeing into the core of me.

"I want you to teach me to fence."

Mr. Jones spins, walks away.

"It's you, isn't it? Arden Jones, Olympian."

I trail after him. Mr. Jones ignores me, positioning sports equipment for the after-school program.

"Please. I need to fence."

No answer. Scowling, Mr. Jones moves deliberately, twisting, turning to avoid my gaze.

"You were good. Really good."

"Go home, kid. You're interfering with my work." He stands tall; his face, a scowling mask.

———

Next day, I take the train, then the bus. I wear my hoodie beneath my down jacket. Headphones cover my ears. My body rocks. Rap matches my pulse. Rhymes call out the world's haters. Since jail, I understand the counterpoint beats better than ever.

I can't give up. I can't.

I glimpsed Mr. Jones's inside self. (So different from his body.)

To be black in the seventies, to be a fencing Olympian... (I can't imagine the dedication and courage.)

Seems right Mr. Jones (and only Mr. Jones) should help me defeat Alan.

On my journey, the world goes from mostly white to browner to brown to brown and black. From Newton to central Boston to Mattapan. From rich neighbor-hoods to poorer and poor. From houses with lawns to luxury apartments to small, ramshackle homes and Housing Authority apartments.

I turn off my music. Walk for five blocks listen-ing to people talk. Creole. French patois. Spanish. A Jamaican lilt. I'm soothed.

I go from being worried, on guard, to feeling ease as more people's skin resembles mine.

I pull open the Boys and Girls Club metal door. The woman behind the counter has her hair wrapped in a red-flowered scarf. She nods like she remembers me.

I head straight to the gym.

Mr. Jones has balls, rackets, nets out. He pushes a wide broom to clean the floor. Back and forth. Back and forth, he moves down the gym floor.

He doesn't look up, but I know he sees me.

I can't help thinking: *How come you don't still fence? How come you run after-school programs? Why aren't you famous?*

Once the floor is swept, Mr. Jones applies tape to mark on the floor a smaller basketball court, a foursquare court, and a dodgeball area. It must get crazy claustrophobic having lots of kids share space. In the corner, there are multicolored jump ropes. I can't imagine there's enough room for double Dutch.

Though I'm not speaking, I'm pleading, *Teach me how to fence.*

Mr. Jones ignores me. Keeps prepping the gym. Weird, how most times I don't want Middlefield Prep students to see me; but it would mean so much if Mr. Jones would see me, teach me to be like him. Not like him now. But when he fenced.

The web says Arden Jones had "speed, agility, intelligence to outsmart most opponents." He was expected to win a medal at the Olympics but didn't. Why not?

School's out.

Kids start to pour in, laughing, yelling, dashing for the balls. Even though it's winter, most of the kids don't have down jackets and gloves like me. Some only have sweaters, thin jackets; some, no socks, and some girls aren't wearing tights or wool leggings. They might be cold but they seem happy. A few rush, hug Mr. Jones. His smile is like sunshine.

I feel a bit jealous. Why can't Mr. Jones smile at me?

"Who're you?" asks a boy, coming to stand beside me. "A new kid?"

He's tall like Trey but his skin is black marble.

He grins. "I'm Zion."

"And I'm Zarra."

(Twins, I think. Both a bit taller than me. Kind.)

Zarra's beautiful. First time I ever thought that about a girl. Deep brown eyes. A wide smile. Glowing black skin.

I can't think of anything to say. Not even my name.

I glance at Mr. Jones. He's lobbing a ball to a kid beneath the broken hoop.

Flustered by Zarra, rejected by Jones, I leave, feeling hopeless, heading toward home.

———

SUSPENSION: DAY FOUR

The desk lady's nails are now blue. Yellow beads, on the tips of her black braids, clack.

"Third day in a row. You want a membership card?"

"No, I'm good."

She shrugs. "Suit yourself."

I take a step.

"Hey, you're not from around here."

An REI jacket. Beats headphones. And even though I'm not a basketball player, I'm wearing red Under Armour Curry 6 shoes. Sweats with Under Armour blazing down the sides. It's obvious I'm rich enough, or rather my parents are, to pay for a gym.

"I'm Delores." She smiles. "Let me know if I can help." I can tell she means it.

"Thanks. Thanks a lot." I feel hopeful. Maybe Mr. Jones will help me after all.

Mr. Jones works hard setting up the gym for dozens of kids. From the equipment closet, Mr. Jones drags gymnastic mats. Traffic cones fall over. Balls skitter across the floor.

Instead of just watching, I help.

I don't say anything. Neither does Mr. Jones.

I scoop rolling basketballs, placing them on the court down left.

Down right, masking tape outlines two small four-square courts. I place underinflated handballs in the center. "These need air."

Mr. Jones nods. "There's a pump in the closet."

When I'm done expanding the balls, I hear, "Grab the jump ropes."

The ropes are thick, heavy—fourteen feet long for double Dutch. Used to be only girls did it; now boys do, too.

I'm feeling great. Mr. Jones and me are getting ready for the after-school crowd.

"If you want, I could use the tape to make a hopscotch."

"You think there's enough room?"

"Barely. But it's different. Kids might like it. But I don't have to."

"No, go on."

Mr. Jones watches as I diagram in the far corner, squares with black tape.

I murmur, "My mom still plays hopscotch."

"Does she now?"

Now I know he thinks my family and me are weird.

Mr. Jones sits on the wooden bleachers. I glance at the clock. Ten minutes before the yellow school buses arrive, bringing the crowd here.

I sit not far from Mr. Jones, studying his profile. He's all angles. Sharp nose. Bent knees. Back tilting forward. Hands clasped, his arms making a triangle beneath his chin.

"Teach me to fence," I blurt.

He looks at me, same piercing glance as before. But I swear I see his loneliness. (Is he married? Got kids?)

"Why aren't you in school?"

Ashamed, I shake my head. "Why don't you fence?"

"Look, kid. You came to me. You want something

from me. If you want it bad enough, you'll answer my question."

"Then will you teach me to fence?" My foot quivers.

"Depends."

"Then why should I tell?"

"Your choice, kid."

"Stop calling me 'kid.'" I feel conflicted, confused. My leg bounces uncontrollably. Jones is studying me. Making decisions about me. This makes me even madder.

"Take a breath. Hold it. Three seconds. Then blow through your mouth."

I don't know why I do what he says. But I do.

"Again. Breathe in through your nose. Count to three. Exhale through your mouth."

Whoosh.

"Again."

One-two-three.

"Feel better?"

I nod. My leg's still. Knots untie in my stomach.

"Headmaster suspended me."

"What?"

"The headmaster suspended me."

"For what?"

I stare at the gym floor, wondering if I *really, really know* why McGeary suspended me? Sure, my skin is black. Racism. But what did McGeary *really, really feel* about punishing me? Why was he quick to write me off?

Mr. Jones stands over me. "Kid, look at me."

I look up, sitting straighter, but it's no use. Jones towers over me. I feel small, insignificant.

"Did you hurt someone?"

"No."

"Did you threaten someone?"

"No."

"Have a weapon?"

"No, sir," I say, leaping up. "I would never."

"Disrespect?"

"Mom and Dad taught me to be respectful."

"Talk back? Be arrogant?"

"I was upset. The headmaster might've thought I was arrogant. But I wasn't. I was trying to explain I didn't do wrong. Even though a teacher thought I did."

"Where you go to school?"

"Middlefield Prep."

He whistles. Then, says, walking away, "You'll be fine."

"That's it?" I ask, bewildered. "You're not going to teach me?" My voice gets louder as Mr. Jones walks farther downcourt.

"Fence at Middlefield," he snaps.

"They'll never give me a chance." Anger wells, sickening me. I can't forget. The handcuffs. Car ride. Jail.

"Headmaster called the police," I shout. "They came. Took me away. Didn't even call my parents." Terror comes back; I smell vomit and bleach.

The prisoners still haunt me. Some might've broken the law. But what if one of them was innocent? A grown-up version of what happened to me?

I'm nauseous, furious.

The room spins. What if I'm jailed again?

I rush toward the door, feeling stupid, angry that I ever thought Mr. Jones could help me.

"Kid." Jones clutches my arm.

I jerk it away. "Don't call me 'kid.'" I realize catching

me, Mr. Jones must've moved like lightning. He's not winded. Didn't even break a sweat.

"What's your name, then?" His voice is soft.

"Donte. Donte Ellison."

I don't breathe. Sweat beads on my neck. (Please, please, say yes.)

Mr. Jones frowns; his eyes glaze. He's not seeing me. He inhales, exhales while shaking his head.

"Help me." (I surprise myself. I'm not begging. Just saying what I think he should do.)

He grimaces, refocuses on me.

Blank-faced, I don't move.

"Be here Saturday, 8:00 AM sharp. A minute late, it's over. No second chances."

"Won't need a second chance."

Mr. Jones extends his hand.

We shake. For seconds, he squeezes hard to make sure I understand. I squeeze firmly back.

Mr. Jones smiles. Just a little bit. Like he doesn't want to seem too encouraging.

But it's enough. I'm happy.

First time since being suspended.

66

2
TRAINING

FIRST POSITION

I arrive cold, bleary-eyed, excited.

I slipped out of the house at 6:00 AM. Train. Bus. Walk.

Mom and Dad are probably reading the note I left on the kitchen counter.

> Don't worry. Be back soon.
> DONTE

Knowing Trey, he's still snoring, sleeping. Probably dreaming of dunking hoops.

I stomp the snow off my shoes. Five minutes to spare: 7:55 AM.

Before I even pull the door handle, I hear locks clacking. See Mr. Jones in sweatpants and a T-shirt.

"Come on in."

I follow him into the gym. He turns on the lights, ups the thermostat. Then, he studies me. I feel awkward. Pinned like a bug. Standing while Mr. Jones walks in a circle around me, his head nodding, occasionally grunting, then humming. "Mmmmm. You're small."

I square my shoulders. "So?"

"Don't puff up. It's good. Means you're less of a target."

"Really?"

"Yes. You have to learn how to fence anybody—large, small, tall, short. You're wiry."

I blink.

He squeezes my biceps. "Or at least you could be. Tight, taut, controlled. Give me ten push-ups."

"Now?"

"Yes, now."

I unzip my jacket.

"No, now."

I hit the floor, arms and legs outstretched.

"Plank position. Good. Hold it a second, then start."

My elbows bend, my body lowers. I push up. My open jacket scrapes the floor.

"Hold for a second. Down," he barks.

Down. I don't think I can push back up. My arms quiver. Up.

"Again."

My whole body trembles.

"Again."

I grit my teeth.

"Again. Don't hold your breath."

I puff air, trying to power through.

"Again."

I collapse.

"I can't."

"Isn't any 'can't.'"

"Mr. Jones," I complain, rocking back on my heels. "I really can't."

"Coach," he says sharply. "To you, I'm Coach. Not Mr. Jones. Not Jones. Coach."

His body seems easy, relaxed, but it's his eyes that are speaking, daring me to quit, to give up.

My jaw tightens. I do a plank. Another push-up. Fast, then another. And another. My arms and back are on fire. Mr. Jones—Coach—thinks he can make me quit? What kind of coach is he anyway?

I won't quit.

My hands and feet dig into the floor. Push. Push.

"Enough," he orders.

"No." Focusing beyond pain, I lower my body, almost touching the floor, then push. "Ten," I shout, holding plank position, showing him, Coach, I'm controlled, strong. "Ten."

Mr. Jones squats, helps me up.

My body's Jell-O. Legs wobbly, arms dangling. Sweat drains on my face and chest. I throw down my jacket and hoodie. "That was awful."

"It's about to get worse." Coach chuckles.

He's happy. I don't believe it.

"You just showed how much you want it. I can teach a lot of things. But I can't teach drive."

I smile. Mr. Jones—no, Coach! My coach. Really, truly!—is transformed. Smiling wide like he's the luckiest man. He slaps me on my back, and I stumble forward.

Coach chuckles again. "Sorry, kid."

"Donte, Coach."

"Yes, Donte."

We look at each other. I feel like we're speaking in silence.

I'm thinking, He's really strong. He's an Olympian. He's thinking (I think), I can teach him all I know.

Then it hits me. I've never had a coach before. Never wanted to do anything where I needed one.

"It feels good," I say aloud. (Having a mentor.)

Coach's smile fades. "Then I mustn't be doing my job. Squat. Give me twenty. Butt out, back straight."

I squat.

"One." Coach counts down. "Two. Three—"

Inside me burns—not angry—a blazing, comforting fire.

I can do this. I didn't know I could do this. Be physical.

Licking sweat from my upper lip, I admit I

like having Coach. Like feeling crazy-exhilarated, exhausted.

"Eighteen, nineteen. Twenty."

"What else?" I say. "What else you got?"

"Be careful what you wish for," Coach deadpans. He's intense, focused.

I'm not scared.

Bring it.

Who knew? Donte Ellison, athlete.

CAN'T MOVE

Misery. I can't move. Put me out of my misery. Every muscle in my body aches. My legs, my shoulders, my back. The soft bed even hurts. I'm going to lie here forever.

"Hey." Trey smacks me with his towel.

"Ouch."

"What's with you?"

"Mr. Jones. Coach, I mean," liking the shape of the word in my mouth. I moan, sitting up.

"You found him? Why didn't you tell?"

How to explain that I wanted to keep the secret close? Wanted it to be mine?

Trey grabs my arm. "You've got to move. Stretch."

"Let me go." Aw, my legs hurt. I want to punch Trey.

"I know this, Donte." He drags me onto the floor. "Stretching is key. Gets you ready for the next workout. Okay." He nods. "Legs in front, fingers stretching toward your toes."

Another coach.

"Just be gentle," says Trey. "In a bit, it'll feel good. Like your hamstrings sighing."

"You're nuts." I laugh. But I do what Trey says.

"You're a *Minecraft* couch potato."

"True."

"You'll get hurt going full out too soon."

"Tell that to Coach."

"Now pull one leg up, foot touching knee. Stretch forward again."

I do it. Trey does it with me.

"What's he like?"

Arden Jones. Trey doesn't have to say the name.

"Complicated," pops out of my mouth.

"Like you," says Trey.

"No I'm not."

Trey shrugs. "Other leg."

The bedroom door opens. It's Dad.

"Pancakes?"

Trey and me raise our brows.

"I'm cooking."

Good. Mom's pancakes are lumpy.

"You boys working out?"

"Donte's fencing. With a real Olympian. Arden Jones. I'm helping him."

I keep my head bowed, looking at my bent knee. I wish Trey hadn't told.

"Is that where you were yesterday? That's why the note?"

"Yeah." I worry Dad's mad at me. (Yesterday, after coaching, I went straight to bed.)

"I used to fence."

"You did?"

Dad shines his goofy grin. "In college."

"You went to Cornell, didn't you? All white."

"Not entirely," says Dad. Then, sheepishly, "Mostly, especially back then."

(Figures.)

"I took ballet, too."

Trey and me crack up. Dad laughs loud. He knows we're seeing him as a clumsy, too tall, skinny guy surrounded by graceful, beautiful girls in pink tights.

"I was the lone guy. Wouldn't be that way now."

"Tights?" chokes Trey, smothering his laugh.

"Black," says Dad, lifting his leg. "Classmates called me Chicken Legs. GIANT CHICKEN LEGS."

Trey and me are rolling on the floor. Pushing, shoving, rolling on each other like little kids. Hilarious. Our dad is hilarious.

"See. First position. I can do first position." Dad puts his heels together, toes pointed out. "Plié." He bends his legs, knees over his toes.

Too much. Trey and me rush, tackling him. We're all on the floor, wrestling, laughing, yelling. Dad's calling us rug rats.

I'm breathing heavily. When did we stop playing like this?

I jump up. "Fencing first position is different."

I show what Coach taught me. "Legs at a right angle. Right foot forward, left foot back and perpendicular. Knees bent. Strong core. Strong balance to move forward or back. To strike or defend."

"Yes, I remember," says Dad, positioning himself. "Line up."

And we do. Dad, the tallest; then Trey; then me. Lightest, lighter, dark.

All squatting, imagining a sword is in our hands. *On guard.* Ready to take on the world. Ready to fight.

"What's that saying?" asks Dad. " 'All for one?' "

"Three Musketeers," Trey answers. " 'All for one. One for all.' "

Family. That describes family.

Dad, Trey, and me.

Four.

"We've got to add Mom," I say.

Dad and Trey nod.

Mom is queen. We're her defenders.

Mom defends the needy, the poor. "Social justice," she says.

I won't be needy. I'm not poor.

I'll defend myself against Alan.

BACK TO SCHOOL

Dad drives Trey to school first.

"Trey's preparing a surprise for you," Mom says. "I'll drive you."

It also means Mom wants to talk private with me. I bite my toasted bagel. It tastes like cardboard. I'm already nervous about returning to school. Mom doesn't play. She's a fighter.

"I want to file a civil rights case. For you, and other students of color who are punished disproportionately."

" 'Disproportionately?' What's that mean?"

"Means all over the country there's a pattern of

brown and black kids receiving harsher school punishments than white students."

"You mean like going to jail?"

Across the kitchen table, Mom clasps my fingers. "Yes. Massachusetts Board of Education."

"Like *Brown v. Board of Education*?"

"Except state, not federal. With an emphasis on private, independent schools. Tuition or no tuition, you shouldn't have been discriminated against." She leans toward me. "Donte, can I make you lead plaintiff? Can I do that?"

I study Mom's nails. Clear, no polish at all. Why can't I be a regular "don't bother me" kid?

I squirm. I thought I wanted to sue Alan. But it would really be his parents. It's Alan I want to battle. Not his parents, the state of Massachusetts, or private schools. Besides being plaintiff, I'd be visible to the entire school, city, and state as "that kid."

But I'm already living forever on the internet. Donte Ellison, handcuffed, prodded by police.

Still—I know if I say no, Mom won't file the suit. Or else she'll find another kid to spotlight. Either way, she won't hold it against me.

I sigh. In Brooklyn, I thought I was "normal." But somehow, I'm not quite "normal" in suburban Massachusetts. Maybe I fooled myself about New York? Maybe I just didn't want to believe racism was there, too? Or just hadn't had it directed at me?

"Yes. Make me the lead." Too late for me to be invisible. Maybe it's sick that I ever thought I could be?

I'm Donte Ellison. Deal with it.

Mom pulls me up from my chair, hugs me. She smells like roses. Then she holds me, arm's length. Eyes focused on mine, she wants me to understand.

"Donte, you'll have to appear in juvenile court." Her voice wavers. "It's different from the civil case. You'll still have to answer for Middlefield Prep's delinquency charges."

Can I curse? Shout? Punch? Run away from the world?

"It's okay, Mom. I'm ready." At least, I think I am.

Middlefield is like a resort. Arching trees, heavy with snow, open spaces with benches, bushes, and winter-quiet plants. The redbrick buildings are covered in vines, which will bloom green ivy in the spring.

There's a crowd in front of the main building. Our car enters the circular driveway and my leg starts bouncing and my insides burn. (Gone a week but it feels like years.)

Trey waves. The entire basketball team is beside and behind him, and they're waving, too. Cheerleaders are jiggling pom-poms, wearing royal-blue-and-white tops and short skirts. (They must be FREEZING.) They chant: "Go, Middlefield Prep. Go, Donte Ellison. Go, go, go." It's the stupidest cheer ever.

Mom smiles; my leg stills. I leap from the stopped car.

Trey fist-bumps me.

Coming back isn't as hard as I expected.

"How'd you do this?" I mutter in Trey's ear.

"Simple. Ellison brothers stick together. No one can be my friend without being yours."

"Could've done this sooner."

Trey pulls back. "Yeah. But I shouldn't have to. Kept hoping kids would see how fly you are. Just you. Nothing to do with me." Trey hugs me, thumping my back. (Is he comforting me or himself?)

I shrug. "Fake is better than hate." (I don't mean that.)

"Complicated," both Trey and me say. (Perfect understanding.)

The bell rings. Everybody starts walking into the building. Dylan taps my arm. "Sorry, Donte. I felt bad when you were in the office. A lot of us did." Then he scoots away, turns, waves before disappearing into the crowd. Amy, Beth, and Claire (aka the ABC Girls), who always hang together, smile and wave.

I feel hopeful. Middlefield Prep might work.

"Got game, little brother. Girls are going to be calling you."

"Quiet, Trey." Problem is I won't know if they like me for me. Or because they like Trey.

(Zarra would like me for me.)

I don't see Headmaster McGeary. Mr. Waters is standing in front of the office door. He nods.

I shiver. I never want to go inside that office again.

To the right, I see six masked fencers. It's got to be Alan; his lieutenant, Danny; Brent; Dave; Marvin; Josh. It's not fencing season, but the white-suited figures intimidate.

Behind the mesh, I imagine Alan glaring.

He hates me.

I shudder. (I'm not used to being hated.)

The bell rings again. Everyone starts racing to class. Behind me, I hear a roar like a windstorm racing, raging.

Bam. I fall flat on my face.

Each teammate gets a dig, a stomp, a step on me. Trey is flailing, trying to shove them away. Mr. Waters is gone.

Alan and his teammates squeal, chuckling loud and high-fiving. In a flash, they're gone. Disappeared around hall corners into classrooms.

Unsteady, I stand.

Trey says, "Sorry." He clasps my hand. "I'm always saying sorry."

"At least Mom didn't see."

We smile grimly. We've got a secret.

The final bell rings.

"See you after school." Trey's fist taps his heart, then he fist-bumps me, and struts away quick.

I'm late for class. My right wrist feels achy, twisted. I hold it close to my chest, walking down the wood-paneled hall with photos of headmasters—all male, all white—looking down on me. Maybe some of them would've accepted me? Maybe some not?

I flash on the scene of the students welcoming me. Trey, standing proud.

Dylan said sorry. We both know he saw Alan's pencil hit Samantha. (Maybe he was coming to tell the headmaster?)

I get it. It's hard to go against Alan. But Dylan

must've come to the office to tell the truth. Seeing Headmaster furious, he backed down. Should I blame him?

Yes? No? Strangely, I feel better. How many others are like Dylan? Wanting to speak up but scared? I might've missed some kindness. Or maybe I was supposed to figure out that kindness to Trey also meant me? I'm glad folks are now being nice. But what if Trey wasn't here? What if it was just me?

Prejudice is wrong. Wrong, it makes me doubt people. How else to protect myself?

Yet if Mom and Dad had doubted, me and Trey wouldn't be. (Liking, loving people shouldn't be hard.)

Standing in the long hallway, I want to scream. Then, I do.

Scream.

Why not?

I wait patiently for some teacher or the headmaster to walk me to the office. But no one comes.

What's that mean? I wonder.

I shrug. Head to Algebra Two.

Why can't the world make sense like numbers? A two is a two. It is what it is. Can't be a three. Or a ten. Not even an eleven.

If I were a number, I'd be seven—seven days, seven colors of the rainbow, seven notes on a musical scale, seven continents. Seven seas.

Not "black brother," just seven. Lucky 7. Magical.

ON GUARD

"Advance. Retreat. Advance. Advance. Retreat."

I've been squatting, letting my core be my strength.
First position. Right foot vertical, leads heel-toe, heel-toe
forward. "Advance. Advance." One arm's outstretched.
The other is behind me, right angle. My hand flops at the
wrist.

"Retreat."

Left leg horizontal, heel-toe, heel-toe, slides back.
It isn't easy. Legs have to move fluid.

Coach calls the command and no matter what it is,
I have to be ready. "Retreat. Advance. Retreat, retreat.
Retreat," he shouts.

I stumble. "This is nonsense. Weeks we've been practicing footwork. I don't even have a sword."

"You'll get a sword when you're ready."

"I'm ready."

"You think so?" Coach looks down at me.

If I say yes, Coach will say I'm being arrogant. Proud.

"What're you teaching me? Dancing?"

Coach laughs, hands me a water bottle. "I'm teaching patience."

"What I need that for?"

Coach turns full circle, studying the gym as if he's remembering. Sometimes when he's teaching, he gets dreamy, wistful. If it was me, I'd brag all the time about having been one of the best fencers in the world.

Coach rubs his neck, staring at the gym wall with its dirty windows, covered by bars. "Swiftness, intelligence can win a match. But patience is the real necessary skill.

"Advance," he barks.

I sink into first position. Again. One arm up, the other outstretched, fist balled around a pretend sword.

"Advance. Advance. Retreat."

Coach's voice unsettles me. There's an anger in his voice, but I don't think he's angry at me.

I hold position, eyes forward, as Coach circles me. My thighs are sore, trembling. But I'm in better shape. Trey and Dad have been helping—running, wrestling, stretching with me. Coach has taught me form. Fencer's form. Back straight, sink low, keep your body, the core, strong. Never rock the body. Only feet move, quickly, slowly, backward or forward.

I don't move.

"Keep your eyes on your opponent," Coach has drummed into my head. So, even though nobody's across from me, I keep my eyes and pretend sword fixed.

"Good job, Donte." Coach pats me on the back. "Your dad has a surprise for you."

"My dad?" I straighten.

Coach looks at the wall clock. "Ten. About now."

Trey bursts through the gym doors, lugging long nylon bags. "Dad's parking. I've got the goods."

I rush to help. "What're you doing here?"

Trey says, "Hey, Coach." Dumping the bags, he stretches out his hand. "Nice to meet you."

I study Coach, scared of what he might say. *(Please don't act surprised, ask, You're the white brother?)*

Cool, collected, Coach shakes Trey's hand. "Good to meet Donte's brother."

How'd he know?

"You look just like him."

"That's what I think, too," says Dad, carrying several black vinyl bags.

Coach extends his hand. "Arden Jones."

"William Ellison."

I elbow Trey. He elbows me back.

"Your son has a gift."

"Wait? Wh-what?"

Dad looks proud, but then he's always proud of me.

"My baby brother?" blurts Trey, disbelievingly.

I punch his shoulder.

"Until today, he didn't complain once about not having a sword."

"You kidding me?" asks Trey, shocked. "How'd you fence without a sword? What's it been—?"

"Weeks." Coach grins.

"You did that on purpose?"

Coach ignores me.

I shake my head. Coach outwitted me and I'd been too dumb. *Or had I?* Was he testing my patience?

"Well, the fencing world gets better today," hollers Trey, opening the nylon bags.

Swords. Sleek, long steel swords with curved handles. Treasure. Serious treasure, I think.

"I've got masks, jackets, and gloves." Dad stoops, opening his bag.

I'm overwhelmed. Coach says I've got a gift, and Dad and Trey are here supporting me. In New York, Mom and Dad were always buying stuff for Trey's basketball team. Middlefield Prep doesn't need the help, but that doesn't stop them from cheering, going wild in the stands. Trey's good. A high scorer. Good on defense, too.

"You want to learn how to fence?"

Coach is looking at Trey. I hold my breath. I want to shout: "This is my team," but I don't have a team. There's just me. And Coach. At the Boys and Girls Club every Saturday. *My* world.

Ignoring Trey, I study the wood floor.

"You should do it," Dad encourages.

"Naw. It's Donte's thing."

I exhale, relieved. Trey winks. (Perfect under-standing.) Trey's the best brother. He's the one who reminded me to fight my own battles.

"Donte needs sparring partners. With your height, you'd be perfect."

Trey doesn't look at Coach. I'm surprised. Trey always stands tall, seems confident.

"Well, good thing I invited Zion and Zarra."

Like magic, Zion and Zarra burst through the gym doors.

"Hey," says Coach.

Brother and sister, both lean, taller than me, over-flow with confidence. Happiness, too.

"This is Mr. Ellison, Donte's father."

"You the brother?" asks Zion.

"Of course he is," snaps Zarra.

I want to hug, well, maybe high-five Zarra. Now I know she's special, seeing my brother.

"What's your name?"

"Trey."

My brother smiles goofy. I groan. He thinks Zarra's beautiful, too. If he becomes competition, I'll lose.

"Let's get to work."

Trey and Dad sit in the stands.

"First position," Coach yells. "Zion and Zarra, copy Donte. Feet at right angle. Back arm up, hand flopped over, relaxed. Sword arm straight." He circles us.

"Good. Thanks to Mr. Ellison, we have swords." He lifts a sword from the bag. "A foil."

Then he hands one to each of us. "A foil can be used forever. It is the most basic sword, but don't think it isn't powerful. Great men and women have fought honorably with a foil."

"What women?" asks Zarra.

"Look it up," shouts Coach, keeping focused on the lesson.

"Press your thumb and index finger against the grip. Thumb and finger control the blade. Not your wrist or arm."

My thumb and index finger touch the cool grip. My fingers curl about the handle.

"Lightly but firmly. Fingers—not the wrist and arm—help guide the thumb and index."

I test, trying to point: **Here. There. Up, down. Side to side.**

"Donte, not from the wrist and arm," shouts

Coach. "You don't want to signal your attack." Coach extends his sword. "Watch. Try to guess which way my point tips."

We watch.

It's hard anticipating which direction. You can't see Coach's fingers, and his arm doesn't move. The blade's tip has a life of its own.

Coach's face is tight, drawn, intensely focused. I wonder who he's fighting? Who's his imaginary opponent?

"Your eyes," I shout. "A giveaway. Your eyes shift slightly, ever so slightly toward where you're going to strike."

"Excellent," answers Coach. "Well done." He walks toward me. "What're you going to do when your opponent wears a mask?"

Zion and Zarra laugh.

But Coach is proud of me. He squeezes my shoulder like Dad does.

"Rule number one: See everything. Not just the blade, but the legs, trunk, arms, tilt of the head. Train the eye. Look for the subtle signs. The subtlest of intentions."

Coach kneels; he's kid-size now. He waves Zion, Zarra, and me close. He looks at each of us, one by one. "It's easier to see now. But in a real match, everyone is in a white suit, a white and mesh mask. Hands are gloved. But there's still plenty to see. An excellent fencer sees all.

"That's what you're going to be. Excellent."

" 'All for one. One for all,' " shouts Zarra.

"Show-off," quips Zion.

Zarra grips my hand, Zion's hand—and lifts them high. "Champions."

"How do you know?" I ask.

Zarra drops my hand, points. "Coach. We've got the best coach."

Grinning, Coach shakes his head. "The Black Count is the man."

I like how Zarra talks direct, believing every word she says. As though believing alone makes anything true.

Arden Jones *is* the best coach. (Who's the Black Count?)

"On guard!" Coach yells, rising. "The call for your opponent to prepare to defend themselves." He sinks down into first position. "This is your power start for both offense, defense. All action stems from this core strength.

"Line up."

Me, Zion, and Zarra position ourselves.

"On guard."

Our knees bend, our torsos lower. Left arms pull back. Our right arms extend.

Quickly glancing at Zion and Zarra, I admire their intensity, focus. Separate from me; yet, we're all together. I get an inkling of why Trey likes sports. Team. Teamwork. A different kind of family.

Dad, elbows on his knees, is relaxed, happy. Leaning forward, Trey's expression is intense, watchful. Hungry. What's that mean?

Coach yells; I move. "Advance. Toe to heel. Toe, heel."

I'll enjoy fencing more after I beat Alan. He's my opponent. Always.

On guard.

I advance.

Soon I'll attack.

THE STRIP

The battlefield is a mat—forty-six feet long by six feet wide. Unlike the movies, you don't dash, leap, run wild. There's a grace to fencing. A grace contained on a small strip, forcing you to fight. There's no quitting the strip. Keep close, keep constant distance between you and your opponent as you advance, retreat.

Always—you're a lunge away from a hit.

RECONNAISSANCE

"You mean spying?"

"No, Donte. Reconnaissance."

"What's the difference?"

"Spying is when you go undercover. Be secret. Reconnaissance is scoping out the enemy on their home turf."

"I don't know, Trey."

Truth is I don't want to see Alan. School days, I try to avoid him. Except in Ms. Wilson's language arts class, I can't. I sit in the first row where Ms. Wilson can see me and not blame me (again) for something I didn't throw. Alan stays in the back because he rarely does his homework. We coexist.

But striding into fencing practice would be like poking a bear. He'd be furious.

Still, I'm curious. Months of conditioning, jogging, I've seen flowers bloom, trees turn green, and birds' eggs hatch. My body's stronger, muscular. (Have I gained ground on Alan?)

Trey's head tilts. "You aren't scared, are you?"

"You ever known me to be scared?"

"Well—"

"Being arrested doesn't count," I snap.

Trey brushes strands from his eyes. Like Dad, he wears his hair long; sunlight bleaches it blond.

"Never mind, Donte."

We're in the backyard. Eating reheated pizza. Trey's downing a protein shake, trying to act cool. Veins in his neck are strained. I can tell something's not right—but what?

Minority Report. I turn another page. Dad likes to give me old-time science fiction. But the ideas never seem old-time. Philip K. Dick's characters are jailed for crimes before they've committed them. Sounds like discrimination to me. (Who knows what somebody's going to do before they do it?) Supposed to be the future, but seems like now to me.

Trey's shoulders slump; his lips press against one big fist.

"You okay, Trey?"

His eyes are downcast. He's hiding something.

It hits me. "You're already doing it. What's the word?"

"Reconnaissance."

"What a word."

"Dad taught me. It's military. Gathering strategic evidence."

"Spying?"

"Yes."

I'm glad my brother is trying to help. But bothered because, selfishly, I want a sport for myself.

"How'd you get Monsieur Durant to agree? Tryouts aren't until summer."

"Flattered him. Told him the conditioning would help me win another hoops championship. Told him the basketball coach didn't agree. Said 'Fencing is a waste.' "

"Is any of that true?"

"Naw." He swings his feet to the concrete. "But Monsieur Durant fell for it. Upset at Coach. But vain, proud I appreciated his skill."

"I never would've gotten away with that."

Trey looks down. Ants are traveling between cement cracks.

I study him. Everyone thinks he's perfect. Obedient. The "better brother." Makes it easier for him to manipulate, strategize, get special favors. None of that works for me.

Not fair. But it's not Trey's fault.

"Alan doesn't mess with you?"

"Ignores me." Lying on the chaise lounge, Trey's legs seem longer.

"You like it?"

"Yeah. You don't mind?"

(Roles reversed.) "It's a stupid question."

(For years, envious, I watched Trey play sports.)

"I want you to see me." He bats his lashes, puppy-eyed.

I swallow. I should've known Trey would like fencing. He's not fighting for me; yet he's *with* me. Happy, himself, learning a new sport.

"Let's do it."

"Monday?"

I nod. "Yeah." (I can do this, I think. I can do this for my brother.)

Trey laughs, happy I'm going to watch him. I try to swallow dread.

———

I sit in the highest bleacher.

Alan and his crew shout: "Black brother. Look who's here. Black brother, black brother" dozens of times.

I try to telepath, *Be cool, Trey*. He can't hear me. He's hot, steaming mad. (Alan sure isn't ignoring me.)

A furnace roars inside me, too. But I'm trying to tamp it down.

The gym's slick. Nothing old, scratched, or broken like the Boys and Girls Club.

"Gentlemen." Monsieur, the coach, walks down-court. "Line up."

The team is fierce. Six white guys in fencing uniforms. Pants, long-sleeved tops, and cushioned jackets that snap beneath the crotch. Middlefield, in blue lettering, is written downward on the outside of the pants. The school crest: gold, crossed swords, and the script *Non Nobis Solum* are on the jacket back.

Trey's in sweats and a T-shirt. A few other students wearing gym clothes practice, too.

Team tryouts in late July. Hard to get picked since Alan and his teammates have been winning championships since elementary school. Word is Mr. Davies, Alan's dad, pays Durant's salary.

"En garde."

In unison, everyone's feet mark first position. Knees bent, swords outstretched, a seemingly natural extension of the arm, point at an invisible foe. Left arm is back and up at a right angle, the left hand relaxed at the wrist.

Trey looks good. I'm proud of him.

"Bon. Avance, avance. Reculer."

Watching the fencers, I can tell Monsieur Durant said, "Advance, advance. Retreat."

My brother and the team are doing drills. They're beautiful, graceful.

Alan's footwork is perfect. He moves forward, back, keeping his torso upright without once shifting his weight.

My stomach twists. How am I going to compete? Take Alan down? Even Middlefield's worst fencer is better than me. (Though they don't really have a worst fencer. Everyone's good.)

"Avance, reculer. Reculer, reculer, avance. Avance!"

Feet shuffle, slide. A special *shush-shwish* sound.

Monsieur seems like a tiny general, walking up and down the line, making comments, critiques.

I think: All the best fencers are French. *The Three Musketeers* proves it. Monsieur Durant's probably won tons of medals. His team has. Middlefield Prep practices five days a week. State champions two years running. Summers, they're members of a private fencers' club.

Then, there's me. A coach who lost the Olympics (what happened to him anyway?) and stopped fencing.

Saturday practices only. Unskilled sparring partners. No competitions.

Disgusted, I start climbing down. The bleachers creak. Trey twists his head to look at me.

Monsieur yells, *"Attencion!* Ellison, *attencion."*

I sit, sorry I've gotten Trey in trouble. Alan and his teammates are perfectly still—perfectly *en garde.* Up high I can't see their faces, but I know they're smirking.

Me, I'm embarrassed. Angry for both me and my brother.

I can't leave now.

Monsieur Durant pairs off the fencers—two by two. Josh and Brent are first. They put on masks. Suddenly, they look like warriors, kind of like Stormtroopers (but soft cotton instead of hard armor). All the boys hush. Like there's nothing more important than this match.

(A touch is called a point.) First person to get five points wins.

My training sucks.

"En garde." Both opponents in first position, foils balanced, ready to strike.

Monsieur shouts, "Engage."

Then, the two swords touch, cross, making a perfect *X* shape like the school's emblem.

"Engage." The call to action. For seconds, steel slides, pings against steel. Opponents test each other's strength. Slow, slow, tentative...

...Fast, fast. Deliberate, swift motions.

Swords clash, metal clicks, feet shuffle. Advance, retreat. Blades are circling, slipping, sliding off each other. Engaged. Then, disengaged. Always feet advancing, retreating.

So quick. A blur. Josh scores.

In my head, I hear Coach: *"See everything."* How can I see when everything's so fast?

Like Marvel-superhero fast.

I inhale, hold my breath, and exhale. Focus.

See.

And then I see.

Josh makes seemingly out-of-the-blue attacks. Like a shark rushing, attacking. Killer blow. Other times he acts cool, in control, almost refusing to move. The foil tip moves slightly left, then Josh lunges. Another point.

(Only the trunk counts as a point. No hits allowed to legs, arms, or head.)

Josh has two points.

Brent is more cautious. He likes to feint, pretend his sword is going one way rather than another. He tries to psych Josh out, lunging for a hit but really just moving the foil tip slightly while all the time bouncing. Like Muhammad Ali in the ring. Makes it even harder to tell which way he'll attack.

Coach didn't tell me about bouncing. Told me to keep my feet planted.

Bam. Brent gets the point.

En garde.

Touch. Brent's foil touches the jacket just above the heart, bending upward into an arch. Another point for Brent. They take their marks again. Brent advances. His movements are fluid, his muscles like molten steel.

Josh is flustered. He's aggressive, lunging over and over. He's forgotten Mr. Cool.

Brent parries. Parries again. Knocks Josh's blade sideways. Parry, parry, parry. Staccato, light metallic *clangs*. After each block, Brent retreats with quick, small steps. Taunting Josh to attack.

Josh lunges again.

Brent's blade parries, then TWISTS under Josh's foil. LUNGE. It's a hit. A touch.

On guard, Josh breaks form. The space between his feet has shortened. His core is unbalanced; worse, his weight isn't even between his legs. His feet won't be able to advance or retreat smoothly.

Attack. Another hit. *Bam.*

Time's running out. Score: four to two.

The strip confines them. Two masked, white-uniformed fencers. Their feet and foil arms make the smallest possible motions. Except during the attack. With fierce, sudden grace, Brent's arms extend while almost simultaneously, he straightens his back leg as his front foot skims forward.

It all took less than five minutes. Score: five to two.

Wow. Oh, wow. Wow. I clasp my hands atop my head.

I see. *I see.*

Fencing isn't just motion, it's tactics. Mind games.

Brent's seeming passiveness unnerved Josh. Brent toys with him—most times retreating, but then adding a bounce to quicken his speed for a lunge, then hit. Making it impossible for Josh to figure out when to strike back, parry. Soon as Josh reacts, Brent changes course.

Whoever attacks first has right-of-way. The second fencer can't attack until he parries. Then, he can counterattack. Try for a touch. Or not.

Brent baits Josh, letting him right-of-way over and over. Then, unpredictably and quick, he counterattacks.

Strategy. Tactics.

Watching, I'm learning.

Form, you need it for strength, mobility. Don't signal, don't give your moves away. Use tiny movements, then a swift lunge the other fencer can't avoid. He can't block the blade, or he blocks it but can't score.

Fencing is in the body, but it's also in the mind.

Head exploding, I can't wait to talk with Coach.

"Hey, Trey. How about a match?"

My head jerks to the right.

Looking impressive, Alan saunters toward Trey. Curly black hair, blue eyes, he looks like a hero. Trey's wavy hair escapes his ponytail; he looks like a slob. If this were a movie, Alan would win. But Trey's always been a good athlete. He's used to winning, especially basketball.

Still, I want to tell him no. Don't take the bait.

I look at Monsieur Durant. Trey does, too.

Alan exclaims, "I challenge you."

He sounds pompous, I think. Sounds like "I'm honorable" and "You're a coward if you don't accept." But it's a cover. Alan's just being a bully.

He knows Trey is outmatched.

Monsieur shrugs. No dishonor in accepting a match.

I want to scream "Not fair." Trey's going to lose.

How does a few weeks of fencing compare with a champion's years?

"Scared?"

Trey acts like he's on the basketball court. "Come on. Let's go. Toe-to-toe."

I groan. This isn't a free-throw competition.

Alan doesn't even bother putting on his mask. "Monsieur, will you judge?"

"*Oui.*"

"I salute you," says Alan, holding the foil straight up before his face, then he sweeps it down. *Whoosh.*

Trey mimics Alan. Holds his blade, then swings it down.

"*En garde.*"

Trey's barely in position when Alan attacks. A straight thrust.

"Point one," shouts Monsieur.

Alan's teammates are applauding, some even whistling. It's rude. Unsettling when fencers need to concentrate. Neither Alan nor Monsieur seem to care.

Trey glances toward me.

I raise a fist.

On guard.

Disaster. Complete takedown of Trey, my brother, King of the Basketball Court.

Trey leans as he lunges, toppling him off-balance. Alan's sword point hits him easily.

Trey recovers. His positioning is strong, balanced. But he can't move fast enough. Retreat, retreat, retreat.

"Come on, Trey," I holler. (Mistake.)

Alan's boys start chanting, "Alan, Alan. Beat him, Alan."

Monsieur, arms folded across his chest, is amused. *Boys will be boys.*

Sweat on his brow, Trey thinks about one last attack. His face is pinched, focused. Angry, too. I can tell—his lips get super thin like Dad's, like mine.

My body feels wild. Standing, shifting from foot to foot, hands clenching, unclenching. Fury overtakes me. *Tamp it down.*

Trey gets control of himself. His form is perfect.

(Advance, advance. Lunge. *A hit*, I think. *Going to be a hit.*)

Alan shifts sideways. Trey, overextended again,

almost falls. Catches himself. Relentless, Alan lunges toward him, again and again.

Retreat. Retreat. Retreat. Trey loses all form. Alan keeps pretending like he's going to strike. Finally, Trey's feet get tangled, mixed up, and he falls backward.

I think: This is how hyenas laugh. No, I'm not being fair to hyenas. This sound is harsh, rumbling, and staggering. Not a funny laugh at all—but warriors' shrill I-defeated-you laugh.

I run, leaping down over bleachers. "Not fair," I yell. "Trey hasn't been fencing for years."

I stand beside my brother.

Like there was a fencing strip between us, me and Trey face off with Alan. Then Alan's teammates assemble beside him. Six against two.

No one speaks.

Monsieur walks toward his office.

Me and Trey mirror each other—furious, wanting respect.

SORRY

"Both of you? Both of you?" Mom's furious. "How's it possible that I get a call from the headmaster about both of you? Both of you!"

In the dining room, Trey, Dad, and me sit quiet, cowed.

Mom's like a hurricane and there's no way to stop her outrage until it's blown over.

Invisible, underneath the table, my right foot is trembling uncontrollably.

"You'd think I'm raising knuckleheads. No sense. No sense at all. You should be avoiding folks like Alan."

"Hard to avoid students who hate us," I blurt. "Hate me."

Mom glares.

My finger traces patterns on the blue place mat.

"Bullies are everywhere. But facing off? You do not face off less you want to get suspended." She swallows. "Or killed."

Underneath the table, Trey smacks my thigh. We get it.

But Mom doesn't understand how things are different for guys. She'd argue it shouldn't be, but it *is*.

Dad's sympathetic. *He knows.*

The whole world says a man has to be strong. Tough. Even Dad acted tough when he picked me up at the police station. He didn't smile nice, shirk or back down, shake that officer's hand like they were friends.

I know toughness isn't the be-all. Sometimes it's tougher to talk things out. To walk away. Problem is—what if Alan and his crew don't know that? *Smackdown.*

Besides, Alan never would've challenged Trey if he weren't my brother. I feel guilty. What was I supposed to do? Not stand by him when he was humiliated? I had to stand by Trey. We had to stand together.

Dope. Ellison brothers, united.

Mom gulps, then slumps into a chair, crosses her arms on the table, and buries her head.

Us guys jump up.

Dad hugs Mom, his cheek touching her hair. My hand strokes Mom's arm; the other embraces Dad's back. Trey wraps his arms around me and Dad, his head on Dad's back. We're tangled with love.

"Mom, we didn't hurt anybody. We'd never," murmurs Trey. "I fell. Donte helped me up. The others were spoiling for a fight."

"Where was Monsieur Durant?"

"He called the office."

"Trey and me didn't move. Never lifted a hand. I swear, Mom. I swear."

True, we stared mean. Trey and me can't "turn the other cheek" every day. (Can we?)

But Mom is crying uncontrollably. She stands, clutching me so hard it hurts. Her tears wet my neck and shirt. I see Dad and Trey looking at us helplessly.

I understand. (Another twist.) Dad and Trey acting tough isn't as scary. Me, I might get killed. I shudder. (Is this only going to get worse as I get older?)

Contradictions rattle, hurt my mind. (Be tough. Don't be tough.

Don't be tough, get bullied.

Be black, tough can get you killed.)

I shake my head. Bullies, prejudiced, ignorant people make life hard.

Alan's all three: a prejudiced, ignorant bully. Problem is: He doesn't think he has to be better. Do better.

No solution. (Only danger for me.)

"The boys aren't suspended," Dad explains. "Headmaster gave a caution. He's going to speak with Alan, too."

"Alan threatened us," says Trey, defending me.

Mom wipes her tears.

"Monsieur Durant's at fault, too," I add. "He never should've allowed such an uneven match. Sorry, Trey."

"It's okay. Say it. You're the better fencer. I'm proud of you. Bet you could've taken him, Donte. Who knew? My little brother, the fencer? On guard!" Trey pretends to swing a sword.

Mom, Dad, Trey laugh. Happy I've found a sport. Happy I've stopped begging for notes to get out of gym class.

But I'm not happy.

I'm not sure I could've beaten Alan. I might've been as bad as Josh. Though better than Trey.

Today, like a miracle, I could *see* fencing clearer than I'd seen anything before. Both matches took minutes, yet, *seeing*, I was in a zone where time slowed.

I could see present positioning and guess an attack before it was launched. Amazingly, I sensed future moves, too—defensive parries.

I could see each fencer's strengths. Vulnerabilities. *See*, instinctively glimpse, their minds working.

Tactics.

Fencing isn't just slapping foils, it's lightning-speed decisions. Thinking in a split second about possible reactions to one decision and how it affects decisions afterward. Remembering who has right-of-way.

Athletic chess. Except the player isn't sacrificing a

pawn to attack a king, it's a parry, a feint, a foil shift to divert attention.

Excitement rushes through me. Is this my super-power?

My hands clench. *Seeing* is not the same as being able to execute. Josh lost because he stopped thinking, doubted himself. Trey was overconfident. Couldn't help believe he was great, three-pointer-basketball great. (Wrong sport.) Not playing another sport, I can *see, feel* the foil's power.

Maybe I'd have an edge to beat Alan after all?

Mom says wearily, "I'm still scared. What if the judge finds out? Another strike against Donte.

"I'm scared."

Dad pulls Mom close.

Having Mom admit fear shocks Trey and me. We know Warrior Mom gets scared. It's where she draws her strength from, her fighting spirit. But we're not used to Mom saying it *out loud*.

It's a bad omen.

I feel deflated. I'll never stop being angry. I'll never beat Alan.

"It's okay, Mom," I comfort, fibbing to make her feel better. "Everything's going to be okay."

Mom strokes, pats my cheek. I can barely breathe. "Donte," she says, somber, "your hearing is Monday."

Middlefield College Preparatory School
v. Donte Roman Ellison

If I were a volcano, I'd erupt.

PARRY

A fencer attacks—lunges.

His opponent blocks—parries.

Parry as soon as the attack begins or at the end, when the fencer is vulnerable with his foil arm fully extended.

A *detached parry* uses the wrist, snapping fingers, and the blade's flexibility to deflect. A *nonresisting parry* channels the energy of the attacking blade into a circular motion, turning aggression back against the opponent.

The human trunk can be attacked front or back. For the successful fencer, deciding when and which parry to use is the ultimate physical and mental skill.

TEAMWORK

Saturday, Trey and me show up at the Boys and Girls Club. We're both carrying gear—foils, gloves, and masks.

Coach barks, "Boys, two seconds more, you would've been late."

Trey grins. "Yes, Coach," he says, off-balance, lugging his gear toward Zion and Zarra.

Welcoming Trey makes Coach great. He doesn't ask questions: *Why didn't you start before? Why are you starting now?* He just accepts Trey like he's always been training with us.

I want to hug Coach. High-five him. Instead, I say, "Right on, Coach" as the four of us scoop up our foils and line up.

"On guard. Advance. Retreat."

Neighbor kids like to watch. During the week, Coach offers lessons after school. Saturdays, though, are for us three—Me, Zion, and Zarra—now, four, my brother, Trey.

"Retreat. Retreat. Advance. Lunge. Recover."

Coach drills us for thirty minutes. Then he introduces new skills.

"Parry. A different parry for each part of the trunk."

Zion and Trey. Me and Zarra.

Zarra's good. Between moves, she bites her lips, but she's assertive and I have to be quick, defending. While I can see Zarra thinking, her moves are fluid. But I'm better than Zarra. I see her and most times know (maybe even before she does?) which quadrant she's going to attack.

Parry two...three...four.

We're both better than Zion and Trey, who know the moves but do them slowly, hesitantly. It's not second nature like it is for me and Zarra.

"Water break," shouts Coach.

"I've got a surprise," shouts Zion, running to the wood bleachers. He opens a wicker basket. "Jerk chicken," he says, beaming proudly. "I cooked it."

Zarra passes out napkins. "Zion cooks like a wiz. I prefer to be outside. Can't stand the kitchen."

"Neither can my mom," then add, stupidly, "but she likes hopscotch."

"Really?" Zarra stares at me.

I'm tongue-tied. Trey saves me. "Sometimes Mom still plays. 'It's not about the hopping. It's about changing direction,' she says, 'balancing on two feet or one, being focused, scooping up your token, no matter what.'"

Zarra's brows arch.

She's considering. *What?* (Maybe she's deciding whether to like me?)

"As a kid," says Trey, "Mom imagined the token was her dreams. Graduating high school, then college. Becoming a lawyer."

Everyone's quiet. Fried chicken tickles my nose.

Zarra hands me a napkin and a drumstick. "Maybe we should teach your mom fencing?"

"Yeah," I say. "Mom would be good." (Am I blushing?)

"Terrific food, Zion," says Coach, smiling. "Hot, spicy, perfect."

Trey bites a thigh, then chokes. "Aww, burns. What's in it?"

Giggling, Zarra offers Trey water.

"Onion, garlic, cinnamon." Zion counts on his fingers. "Paprika, allspice, white pepper, nutmeg, thyme, brown sugar, ginger—"

"Ten," shouts Zarra.

"Hot chilies and cayenne," adds Zion, sticking out a thumb and finger.

"Are you kidding me?" Trey gulps more water. "All that on a piece of chicken?"

"Jamaican jerk chicken." Zarra looks at me, daring. "What do you think?"

"Fine," I say, trying not to stutter. (It's the spiciest, most scrumptious chicken.) My eyes tear.

"I thought you'd like it. You run hot like Coach. You're an emotional firecracker."

Astonished, Coach and me look at Zarra.

"It's true," says Trey.

"Only Coach hides it better." Zarra's dimples flash.

"Too true," Zion mumbles, still chewing.

"You kids are too smart for me." Coach laughs.

Everyone's feeling good. We chomp on chicken. Except Trey nibbles, hides pieces in his paper napkin. (I don't tell.)

Sitting, Coach relaxes with his hands behind his head, his back resting on a bleacher. He's not the walled-in man I met before. Content, I think. This moment, Coach seems satisfied, happier than before. Not grim. I think he really likes coaching. Likes me, Zion, Zarra, and Trey.

"Why'd you stop fencing?"

Coach jerks upright, stands ramrod straight, and walks away. Doesn't even take his chicken.

"Told you Coach runs hot," Zarra says matter-of-factly. Zion, Trey, and me are downcast.

I wait. Five minutes, Coach isn't back. Ten minutes.

I feel bad, so I start to search. He's not in the building.

Delores sitting at the reception desk, her nails sparkly silver, points a finger at the front door.

"Thanks." I push the door open. Coach's sitting on the steps, knees apart, his elbows on his thighs. Face is droopy, and though he's looking straight at the street (cars whizzing, people walking, talking, even a vendor selling falafel), he doesn't seem to notice them.

It's like he's here but not here.

He gives a big sigh.

I sit beside him. "Sorry. Didn't mean to get in your business."

"Yes, you did."

"I did." I grin. "Can't help it, I'm curious. You had it all."

"Only seems like that for someone who wasn't there." Coach looks at me, serious. "You're a good kid. Talented. But you've got to be smart."

"I'm smart."

"Not school-smart. Not even street-smart. Self-smart."

"What's that mean?"

"Means you're living for your own best interests. On your own terms."

"Doesn't everybody?"

Coach laughs, plucks a weed growing through a crack on the steps.

I lift my face to the sun. It feels good. Winter's long gone.

Still tasting Zion's spicy chicken, sitting beside Coach, I realize I'm happy. Saturday is the happiest day of my week.

"Why'd you want to fence?" asks Coach.

Happiness rushes out of me as I remember Alan's angular face. His nasty words. Him beating my brother. Showing off that he thinks he's not only better than me, but better than Trey.

My insides heat, my legs bob, and my hands, on my knees, curl into fists. I'm angrier than ever.

"Don't do anything for anyone else, Donte. Do it for you. Only you. That's smart."

He stands.

"Coach, don't go."

(Maybe he hears the nervousness in my voice? Maybe he takes pity on me?)

He sits. The two of us, side by side, on the cool concrete step.

I tell him about Alan. How Alan disrespecting my brother felt worse than him disrespecting me. "It's like pain all over. My hands, stomach, feet. I feel awful."

Coach doesn't speak.

At home, I have to quiet myself. Sometimes not talk. But with Coach I'm babbling, feelings gushing like water.

It feels really good having an adult (other than my parents) listen to me.

"Monday is my hearing. I go before a judge. I've been trying not to think about it.

"Mom hasn't said much. She just says not to worry. But I can tell *she* worries.

"She's going to sue. Not for my case. But for a bigger case—a civil lawsuit—with me and lots of black and brown kids who've been arrested in Massachusetts schools. She says justice might prevail."

"Do you think it will?"

"I don't know. This whole mess is Alan's fault. Me, being petrified, having to go to court not once but twice."

"If your mom wins the lawsuit, will it be Alan's fault, too?"

That stumps me. In a way, yes; in a way, no.

"If justice prevails, would experiencing Alan's prejudice have been worth it?"

Worth it? What does that mean? Alan's hurt me a thousand times over.

"I need to think," I say to Coach.

"Yes, you do."

HEARING

The juvenile courthouse is intimidating. Paneled walls, marble floors, and a high ceiling with a stained-glass image of Lady Justice. Sun shines through, and Lady Justice's scales balancing right and wrong shimmer. She's blindfolded. Does that mean no racial bias?

I like her sword. It's thick, more solid than a foil. More like a gladiator's.

Justice means a fight?

Mom reminded me juveniles can't be criminals. I'm a "delinquent." And juveniles don't have trials but "adjudication hearings."

Still, it's scary. I'm in a suit and tie.

We've been waiting in the hallway all morning. A few other families are waiting, too. Some have babies, toddlers. There are a lot of older folks, too. Parents and grandparents.

The majority of "delinquents" are my color—just some lighter, some darker. There are girls in skirts, dresses, and leggings. Most are boys wearing jeans and T-shirts or khakis and polos. I'm the only one in a suit. Like I'm ready for church. Or graduation.

Languages—Spanish, Yoruba, Swahili, Portuguese— and accents—Jamaican, New England, Southern, even Brooklyn—echo off the marble floor, walls. Some seem old enough for middle school, high school. But a few kids are younger—third, maybe fourth grade.

Waiting, I get more and more scared. It takes all my focus to keep myself still. Un-jittery and pretend-calm. Otherwise Mom, Dad, and Trey might lose it.

Everyone—Rodriguez, Adebeyo, Williams, Brown, Sousa, Jones—waits for their surnames to be called. Then, a father and a dazed son, or four family members and a scared daughter, or parents, grandparents, and a young, bewildered boy stand when called and march into the court as the thundering, huge doors close behind them.

After a few minutes, sometimes five, rarely ten, the door opens again. Some folks come out smiling; others, solemn; still others, crying. The worst ones are those wailing or cursing, especially when they come out without the kid they went in with.

Kids are disappeared.

I'm starting to worry that I might disappear—*really, really* disappear behind the courtroom door.

———

We're still waiting when they recess for lunch. My turkey sandwich tastes like sawdust. Even Trey chews and chews, barely able to swallow bread. Mom and Dad don't even bother unwrapping their sandwiches or ripping open bags of chips.

Familiar sneakers *slap-slap* on the wood floor.

I spin, call, "Coach."

My family greets him. Trey's smile is the biggest. Dad winks. (He must've invited Coach.)

"Thank you for coming." Dad shakes Coach's hand.

It feels so right for Coach to be here. Strange, I didn't even know I was missing him until he got here. I hug him, feeling like a "baby brother" again instead of a seventh grader. Coach's return hug feels good. He smells like the Boys and Girls Club—rubber balls, oiled wood, a whiff of mildew, and the tangy sweat of playing.

The courtroom door opens.

"Ellison," a guard barks. "Ellison."

Mom clutches my hand. She puts on her stern lawyer face. Dad pats my back.

"You got this," says Trey, almost jovial. Like I was playing pickup basketball.

Coach whispers hurriedly, "Heads up. Another strip. Another field. See everything. On guard, Donte. On guard."

I think: Coach is speaking gibberish. Fencing isn't life.

I walk through the huge courtroom door, terrified that I won't walk back out.

Donte's stupid wish fulfilled: Invisibility. Disappeared.

Everything in the courtroom is adult-size and makes me feel small. There's a white guard standing in front of the judge's pedestal. On the right is another white man, balding in a blue suit, sitting at the prosecutor's desk. Mom and me sit at the defense table.

Coach, Dad, and Trey are in the spectator stands behind us. No one is in the jury stand.

"All rise."

Mom pokes me. I stand.

The judge, tall and white, looks like a preacher in his dark robes. His glasses are thick, his features angular, reminding me of a peering owl.

"Everyone except the accused be seated."

I grip the table.

"This is a hearing to determine whether you've violated community moral standards. Do you understand that?"

"Yes. Sir." I gulp. (Even though I don't understand.)

"Your name?"

"Donte Ellison."

"You have representation?"

"My mom."

The judge arches his brow.

"Denise Ellison, I mean. My lawyer's name is Denise Ellison."

"Son of a lawyer?"

"Yes, sir."

The judge looks puzzled, like something doesn't make sense.

"Your school, Middlefield Prep, says you're a delinquent. You threw a pencil and a book bag with intention to harm."

"No!" For the first time, I look right at the prosecutor. He represents the state, not the school. The state prosecutor. Mom told me state prosecutors make sure the state keeps delinquents off the street, to uphold the values of the community. Middlefield Prep doesn't even have to send a representative or lawyer. They don't even have to present evidence. Their evidence is the police report.

But the police wrote down lies. Why's the state defending Middlefield's lies?

How come my words aren't on the judge's papers?

"Proof?" the judge asks the prosecutor.

"His teacher Ms. Wilson and the headmaster, Thomas McGeary, made the complaint."

"Are they here?"

"No."

"Mmm." The judge looks thoughtful. I stand straighter, hoping he'll see me as a good kid.

"You're not asking for the charges to be dropped?"

"No, Your Honor. They seem credible."

"Excuse me, Your Honor. Only credible because they're from a rich, white private school. But my son, the defendant, doesn't lie."

(It's okay, Mom, I think.)

"Massachusetts Board of Education bans disproportionate punishment. But it still happens. Even in private, independent schools like Middlefield Prep." Mom's standing, fierce.

"Mmmm." The judge's brow furrows. "You go to a private school?"

"Yes, sir."

"Scholarship?"

"No, sir," snaps Lawyer Mom.

The judge's face is unreadable, his fingers quickly *tap-tap* next to his gavel.

The judge is Lady Justice. Except he's not a girl. I wish he was. He's not blindfolded either. Yet he's going to swing Lady Justice's sword. Determine my guilt or innocence.

I *see* now... it's a match. Like Coach said. This courtroom, another field.

I get it.

Seeing is intuition, trying to predict strategy. *Tactics.*

The prosecutor has made one attack.

I can tell the judge isn't sure he's made a hit. (My opponent—the real one, Middlefield Prep—isn't here. This gives me an advantage.)

The judge leans forward, his hands clasped together, propping up his chin. He's pondering.

What?

Mom said juvenile judges have lots of discretion. "They don't necessarily weigh evidence, proof in the same way as a criminal court."

Middlefield Prep doesn't have to give proof. (Sucks, I think.)

But until today, I didn't understand how a judge could make a kid disappear. Juvenile detention—that's where he must send them. A lockup. (Is it better than a cell?)

A clock hangs above the judge's stand. 1:07 PM. All morning, I saw how most cases only took less than five minutes (okay, some took ten) but I'm at seven. All morning, families in and out, in and out. We've already hit my lucky number. *Seven.* The more time spent is good.

On guard.

It's not a fair match. (No witnesses allowed. Maybe Dylan could've told the truth? Or Ms. Wilson, cross-examined, could admit she didn't *see* me throw the pencil.) Everything is more or less up to the judge.

Mom's gloomy. She's only had one parry.

Unlike a fencing uniform with a mask covering my face, the judge sees me. Knows a little about my background.

I'm not wearing jeans and khakis, but a suit. My mom's a lawyer. Educated. I'm educated. (Middlefield Prep, no less.)

I *see* it. Plainly *see* it. I'm not who the judge expected me to be. And that's my advantage. It's harder to stereotype me.

My stomach knots. Anger makes my hands shake. (Be cool, I think.) *Patience*, I hear Coach whisper inside my head.

I gaze back at Coach. With his Afro sprinkled gray, a blue shirt with the Boys and Girls Club emblem (white lines resembling clasped hands), and a small potbelly, no one would ever guess he'd been an Olympian.

He's been teaching foil attacks. "The best attack is unexpected."

Do the unexpected.

"Your Honor," I say, nervous and high-pitched, startling everyone. "My dad and brother are right there." I point. Flap my arm.

Trey makes Dad stand with him.

The judge's face brightens with surprise. It's like Dad's and Trey's skin tones are a magic reflector.

It's also a point. An unexpected attack. (The foil tip hits at the heart.)

"And that's my coach."

Another point.

Coach stands, nods at me.

"He's teaching me fencing. Coach Jones used to fence on the Olympic team." (A counter, counterattack.)

The prosecutor, the judge, and the guard in the room are taken aback.

The judge is flabbergasted. "Is that so? Which year?"

"Nineteen seventy-six.

"Donte trains with me at the Boys and Girls Club. Community volunteering beyond Middlefield Prep. He helps me."

Coach has scored a point. (Though there's no tag-teaming in fencing.)

"I used to fence," says the judge. An unexpected point. (And I can *see* the judge connecting Coach, connecting *me* to his school and team memories.)

"It seems strange that a young man like you would get into trouble."

"I would never hurt anyone. Not even in fencing. I always keep the plastic tip on."

The judge chuckles.

Score.

"I didn't throw a pencil at Sam. She's kind to me. I didn't throw my backpack at anyone. I'm here to speak for myself.

"Where's Headmaster McGeary? Why isn't he here to say what I did?"

Match.

The prosecutor caves. "I think the state can drop the complaint."

Mom's lips thin. I see her thinking: *Easy to stereotype kids of color. Especially easier to stereotype poor kids of color. Unfair bias.* (That's her civil rights case. But she's not bringing it up now.)

The judge bangs his gavel. "My judgment: Donte Ellison is not a threat to the community. Nonetheless, he's required to do two hundred hours of service under the supervision of his coach at the Boys and Girls Club of America.

"Good luck."

"Thank you, Your Honor."

Mom hugs me, whispering, "I didn't know there was another lawyer in the family."

Fencer, I think. (Well, maybe a lawyer, too. Lady Justice has a sword.

Why not Donte Ellison, too?)

Still, I don't think the judge's verdict is fair.

Lady Justice is blind. But it mattered to the judge that he could *see* I wasn't poor, *see* I had a coach, educated parents. A white dad, a white-skinned brother.

I look at Mom; she's studying me. Her expression, woeful. Because of how the world *sees,* skin color gives us another bond.

Not fair.

"I love you, Donte."

"I love you, Mom."

CELEBRATE

We're starved. Lunch at Akiko's.

I order miso soup, shrimp tempura, and California rolls with cooked fake crab. I think: Food isn't food until it's cooked. Yet, Mom, Dad, and Trey eat raw fish. Tuna. Yellowtail. Spicy salmon rolls. Coach eats *uni*. He calls it "*oo-nee*." It's spongy-looking, not quite orange or brown, with bumps.

"Ate this in Japan. Decades ago. An international meet. Our team hosts said we had to try." Coach takes a bite, sighs. "This brings back memories."

I've never seen Coach so relaxed. Like he really likes hanging out with our family.

"Can I try one?"

"You sure?" Using chopsticks, Coach sets on my plate white rice with *uni* on top.

Using my fingers, I dip the sushi in soy sauce. "It's sweet," I mumble, chewing, swallowing while everyone watches. "It's good. What is it?"

Dad points at the glass case on the sushi counter. "See the spiny, spindly creature? A round ball with spikes? Like a rolling porcupine?"

"Yeah. It's ugly."

"You're eating its insides," says Trey, barely muffling his laughter.

"Actually, the gonads," adds Coach, "where it breeds eggs."

(Gross.) I smile weakly.

Everyone laughs. Not at me, but with me. I exhale. Then I'm laughing. Tears stream down my cheeks.

From courthouse to *uni*—what a strange day.

RIPOSTE

The riposte is an effective intermediate/advanced skill. Without pausing after a parry, directly thrust and score against your opponent.

Beginners simply parry (defend) or attack (offense). A riposte seamlessly blends the two actions.

A riposte unsettles your opponent, signaling aggression, quickness, and both defensive and offensive power.

3
BOUT

HAPPINESS

Every weekend, Dad drives Trey and me to fencing
practice. He brings snacks and water bottles, not just
for the fencing crew but for everybody. Sometimes fifty
kids. He also bought extra foils. After a morning of
training, Zion, Zarra, Trey, and me teach fencing to the
other kids. Coach supervises. Dad, grinning, watches
from the bleachers.

In the suburbs, most folks look like Dad and Trey.
Here, most kids look like me. At least, color-wise.

Jamil, one of the third graders, points at Trey, asking, "How come you're white? And he's not? Is Donte
adopted?"

"Nope. We're biracial. Our mom's black. Our dad's white."

Zarra stops her lunge. "They're like me and Zion. Sharing genes from the same parents. It's science. DNA. Zion and me were born right after one another. Twins. Me first," she brags.

"Except you're a girl. He's a boy."

"Right. Brother and sister. Not identical."

"Neither are them," Jamil squeaks.

"Yeah," says Trey. "I look like our dad. Donte looks like Mom."

"Oh," Jamil says proudly, figuring it out. "Brothers. Just different colors."

"You've got it, little man," Trey says, grinning. "Donte and me are tight."

Zarra smiles, mischievous. "Yeah. We're all tight."

Zion hoots, high-fives Zarra. Jamil claps. I feel good. Zion and Zarra get Trey and me. Just like we get them. Deep bonds happen all kinds of ways. But nothing's better than brothers and sisters.

"Jamil, let me teach you fencing," says Trey.

"Let Zarra," I say. "She's the better fencer."

"Not," replies Zarra. "Donte's the best. He's *really, really* good."

"Really, really." Trey's fist pumps the air.

Zarra's fly. She totally caught me off guard. Did the unexpected.

Coach studies me. He can tell I'm embarrassed. But happy. I move two steps closer to Zarra. She's the nicest girl I know.

"Show him," says Zion.

Zarra squirms.

"Show me what?"

"I want to see," exclaims Trey, pulling close.

"Can I?" asks Jamil.

"And me?" Dad joins the circle.

Coach watches, too, as Zarra pulls something from her pocket.

"Ooooo," breathes Jamil.

"It's beautiful," I say.

"Milk opal," she says, steady, staring at me. "Popular in Jamaica. Told my mother I wanted a dreaming stone."

Pink, light green, and yellow colors glow against a

soft white. I lift the stone from Zarra's hand. (Perfect for hopscotch.)

"This is for your mom." Zion's fingers balance another opal. "Mom can't wait for our families to meet."

"Our pleasure," answers Dad, taking the stone.

"High five," yells Trey, and we're all high-fiving, fist-bumping, including little Jamil. Only Coach stands off to the side.

Smiling, arms crossed over his chest like a genie, Coach declares, "We're ready for a meet."

ETIQUETTE

A fencing match is called a bout.

Foils swishing downward, two fencers salute one another. Ready to battle, they are, nonetheless, honorable opponents.

The referee calls, "On guard."

Fencers place their masks on and assume proper position, each at their field line.

"Ready?" the referee asks, alerting fencers that the bout will soon begin.

Then, "Fence." Opponents attack and parry.

Bouts are divided into three-minute periods. A match can be a lightning-fast period or five points (touches), whichever comes first. Or whoever scores the most in three periods.

After the contest, the fencers once again salute each other and shake hands. The winner mustn't gloat; the loser mustn't be vengeful.

Mutual respect is a sacred value for all fencers, at every level.

TOURNAMENT

We look smart, slick. Zion, Zarra, Trey, and me. We've got crisp uniforms and the Boys and Girls Club logo on our backs and down the side of our pants.

We're a team. Months of training. Practice bouts.

Coach is super nervous. Sweat speckles his forehead; he paces.

"What's wrong, Coach?" asks Zion. "Don't you think we're going to win?"

"Winning is fine. Fencing honorably is the main thing. Do you remember what I told you about the salute?"

"Yes," I say. "Our opponent, the ref, and the audience."

"Yes," Coach echoes. "Be respectful," he adds, reminding me of my dad. But he's wary, looking around the packed arena, and I don't know why. I can't guess what's wrong. Is he looking for someone? Something?

I start to feel nervous, too. So many teams. So many schools and fencing clubs!

It's only a citywide, preseason meet, but it makes me think of the Olympics. A world of athletes. Excited people in the stands, waving banners and flags.

It's easy for me to spot Middlefield Prep. Its blue-and-gold sword insignia flapping, hanging high.

If I looked down, closer to the floor, I'd see Monsieur Durant and the Middlefield team.

I don't look down. I don't want to see Alan's awful face. But I can't help myself. Across the arena, Alan and his Middlefield crew are staring at me, Zion, and Zarra. Like they think looks alone can intimidate. Zion and Zarra stare back, clasp hands. Trey glares, untangles his headphones.

Coach murmurs, "Fencing has aristocratic roots. But you belong here. We all do."

I study the other teams. Most are six fencers or more. We're just four. I wish we were seven. Then I'd be excited, not nervous. In this arena, fencing seems like a white sport. But that can't be true everywhere, can it? Seems like a private-school sport, too. Oak Grove. Del Haven Prep. Country Day.

Pressure builds in my chest. I *am* intimidated. Not by Alan but because I've never competed in a sport before.

How do players do it?

I'm nervous, thrilled, excited, and anxious all at once. I swallow hard, feeling like I might throw up.

Zarra calmly stretches. Zion looks petrified. Trey, being Trey, bounces his head to a beat only he can hear.

Why didn't I think of that? Music to soothe, distract me.

Girls fence first. There are lots of girls carrying all kinds of blades: foil, épée, sabre.

Makes me wonder why Middlefield Prep doesn't have any girls on the team? I wonder: Is it Alan and his crew's fault? Or Monsieur Durant's? Doesn't seem fair.

Zarra stands at her mark, her braids twisted with ribbons, facing a girl with straight brown hair. The girl seems fierce but nice. Both girls salute each other, the referee, the audience. They put on their masks.

First position. "On guard," yells the referee.

The arena is quiet like church.

"Ready?"

Blades cross without touching.

"Fence."

"Hey, black girl!" A roaring shout.

Startled, Zarra's head turns. She's touched before she recovers enough to parry.

I groan. Though I can't see Zarra's face, I saw her head move left, toward the shout. Zion, even though he knows he shouldn't, is softly cursing.

Trey murmurs, "Come on, Zarra. Come on."

Unlike basketball, football, soccer, there's not

supposed to be any shouting, chattering, or heckling. Nobody knows who made the call. But I do. Trey does.

It could only be Alan.

"Why doesn't the ref restart the match? Why doesn't he, Coach?"

Coach looks down at me. Eyes strained, weary, he says, "No matter what, keep focused. Zarra shouldn't have lost her focus."

Anger bubbles inside me. Coach should be sticking up for Zarra. For the first time, I want to talk back. Tell him he's wrong. He's tough, but he shouldn't be blaming Zarra.

Zarra's off her game. Next point, she wins. A parry, a lunge. Time is ticking and her opponent is good. Zarra's opponent parries then touches the foil tip right above the heart; the foil bends like wire.

Match.

Zarra loses two to one.

Zarra salutes her opponent, walks to our team huddle.

"You okay?" Zarra's mask is still on and I can't see her face. I want to tell her to take it off. Zion shakes

163

his head. I get it. Zarra's crying and she doesn't want anyone to see.

Coach says, "Get some water. Rest."

My right leg lifts onto the ball of my foot, and my heel taps uncontrollably. Remembering chants of "Black brother, black brother," my mouth goes dry. My heart races and I want to scream. Zion has his arm around Zarra. Trey, headphones still on, stares, red-faced, at the floor. I know he's thinking another "sorry." Sorry people can't see we're related, brothers. Can't see skin color is just a shade.

(Trey has my back as best he can.)

But, for the first time, I'm not caring about me. I'm caring about how Alan's shout unsettled Zarra. "Black girl" said with fury and disdain, not kindness and respect.

What if everyone went around shouting out people's skin color? Stupid, stupid, stupid.

What if I screamed "white boy" at Alan?

I know I shouldn't want it—but I want revenge. Not for me, but for Zarra.

Coach watches me. Watches my hands twisting, my head bobbing, my feet jittery.

I think he's going to say something; he doesn't.

Now he's scanning the crowd. I try to see what he's searching for—is it a fencer? Another coach?

(I'm not happy. I think Coach should comfort Zarra.)

———

Deep breaths. In and out. Holding my air three seconds, ten seconds. My body won't calm. I focus on keeping my limbs still.

"Electric scoring is used in regional, national, and international meets," Coach told us. Even though this is preseason, shortened bouts, we're all suited up.

A metallic vest is layered over my jacket. Wires are attached to the button on my foil's tip and behind the silver clasp that protects my hand. Cables attached to me and a reel allow movement. The field is metallic, too.

What if there's a short? And I get *zapped*?

Other bouts—mine included—are about to start. The crowd hushes like a dying breeze. I clench my jaw. Waiting, imagining I'm hearing *Black brother, black brother*. There aren't any shouts.

Still, I'm not all together. The foil feels light in my

hand, which is good; yet, it also feels alien, unnatural. A foil is supposed to be a seamless extension of your arm and hand. Right this moment, I hold it awkwardly, without style or grace.

My opponent is tall, long-limbed. Means his reach—both in his legs and arms—is going to be better than mine.

"Your opponent's size shouldn't matter," Coach likes to say. (Yeah, right.)

We salute the referee, each other, the crowd.

"On guard."

(You've got this, Donte. You've got this.)

"Ready?"

"*Fence*" explodes in my mind and I attack first. The parry, quick, slight, made it seem like the fencer was flicking at a fly.

I lunge again. This time, after a parry, the foil tip touches me, left lower side. The electric scorer flashes green.

A touch hurts. The padded jacket absorbs most but not all of the force.

Mentally, I'm shocked. As if the electric buzzer's light lit up my head instead of the scoreboard.

(Be cool. *See.* Think.)

Time slows, though reality doesn't. *He's going to lunge... the parry is done. Legs and arm shifting, flowing into a lunge, his arm stretching, seemingly forever.*

Touch.

I'm disbelieving. I knew the offense was coming and I didn't do anything.

Time's running out. I don't want to advance or retreat. Three minutes forces both of us not to delay, waver. WE HAVE TO FENCE.

I parry then lunge, my arm stretching for a touch. He retreats. I lunge again and again. Wildly, I lunge; sloppily, the weight between my legs uneven. My opponent doesn't have to engage my blade, just retreat, keep himself safe as the last minute counts down.

Five, four, three, two, one.

Buzz.

All done.

I turn from the court. Wait. I forgot the salute.

I spin back around, salute the referee, my opponent. I shake his hand.

He squeezes it. With his mask off, I can see freckles bridging his nose.

"First match is always hardest," he whispers.

His kindness feels good. We fenced fair and square.

I look across at Coach. Everything feels good. Even though I lost, I realize I *like* fencing.

For a few minutes, the field was the entire world. Nothing else mattered except how my mind moved my body and foil. Everything about me, *in me*, felt tested.

AND IT FELT GREAT.

My opponent fenced fair.

I fenced fair.

Both of us drenched in sweat.

We shake hands. Equals. (That's how it's supposed to be.)

———

Zion, Zarra, and Trey look whipped, beaten.

"Hey, don't be low. We did it."

"Yeah, lost," grumps Trey.

"Doesn't matter. Look around," I say. "No one expected us to be here. We're here. Black kids. My darker brother." I poke Trey.

"Don't joke." Annoyed, Trey brushes me away.

"It's cool, Trey, it really is." I can't explain it. I feel goofy, elated. "Two sets of siblings throwing down."

I look at Zion, Trey. "Be real. You know you liked it." Both crack a smile.

"It was pretty cool," answers Trey.

"Like I was an electric robot," hoots Zion. "With an electric sword."

"What do you know about robots? Electric swords?" Trey and Zion start squawking, chilling, goofing around.

Zarra's still unhappy.

"Zarra," I say gently, "you were awesome." (And I mean it.) "Tough keeping cool. But you didn't give up."

"Yeah, tough."

"Next time, no jerk is going to upset you."

Unbelievably, Zarra hugs me. Then Zion and Trey pile on. We're all hugging.

Teammates.

I look up at Coach. (I get it, I want to say.)

Focus, fence fair, and you're a success.

AFTERMATH

I want another bout. I want to do it again and again and again. I'm thrilled. I feel I can fly. Spin like a hero through the universe. Puff my chest out like a musketeer.

"Mr. and Mrs. Ellison, do you mind taking Zion and Zarra home? I'd like to speak with Donte."

Startled, I look at Coach. (Did I do something wrong?) I crash to earth. My hands clench, unclench; I hide them behind my back.

"Fine with me," says Dad, but his eyes check with Mom.

"See you at home, Donte," she says.

Zarra, gear slung over her shoulder, murmurs, "Don't worry, Donte. It's going to be good, I know it."

Trey punches me. His way of saying *Be tough*.

Zion keeps walking, doesn't turn around, doesn't look at me, just holds his hand up and waves.

Coach stands before me. I stare straight at his tiny potbelly. I don't know why I'm so nervous. (This isn't me.)

No, I know why. Ever since the arrest, I sometimes feel life is going to crash. Out of the blue. Unexpected. But not in a good way.

I don't feel completely safe. (I used to. Not anymore.)

"Doughnuts?" asks Coach.

"Get an old-fashioned. One with sprinkles. What about a chocolate éclair?"

In the pink-and-green shop, smelling of sizzling dough, I get all three. The éclair oozes like mud. Sprinkles look like glittery bugs; even the sugar tastes bitter.

Drinking black coffee, Coach watches me.

"Sorry I lost," I say, eyes cast down.

"I'm not worried about you, Donte. I'm proud of you."

My finger brushes sugar off the old-fashioned.

"I'm especially proud of how you rallied your team."

"Losing is still losing."

"Donte, it's not just about the bout. It's about leadership, giving respect. Patience and control."

I lift my gaze. "You're not mad?"

"Of course not. We're celebrating."

I bite the éclair, loving the chocolate ooze. "I thought I was in trouble."

"Not at all." He leans against the table, his hands folded. "What'd you feel, Donte? When you were fencing?" Coach is urgent, intent like he's holding his breath until I answer.

"It was the best." I exhale. "The speed, the flick of the foil. The rush inside my head."

"You felt alive?"

"Yeah. Like being on a huge screen in high-def. Everything clear, crisp. Even so fast, beyond fast. I knew moves before they happened. I can't explain. Even though I was losing, it felt good."

Coach's hands smack the table. "I know exactly what you mean. I felt the same way."

"You did?"

"I felt unstoppable when I fenced." Sadness shadows his face. Not gloomy but bittersweet. "How about if you be my *padawan*, my young grasshopper?"

"*Star Wars*. But who's a grasshopper?"

"Student in *Kung Fu*. A TV show from when I was a kid."

"You're fooling me. I'm already your student."

"Yes, you are. Today, you reminded me of me. Yet, still without question, you. Watching your focus, your joy, I knew you were born to fence."

Coach's face is eager, happy. Crazy, he glows. He pats my hand. I feel the warmth, the bond between us.

Coach knows what's in my mind. (I say it anyway.) "I want to fence," I say, insistent. "I want to be the best."

The noisy doughnut shop disappears. The cash register doesn't ring. People aren't pointing, shouting, "Can I have that one, please? No, that one. Two." "Two?" "Yes, please." There's only the lasting gaze between Coach and me. (Both of us born to fence.)

"Can I have a taste?" asks Coach.

I tear a bit of the éclair. It's messy. Coach doesn't care. He pops it into his mouth, sighing. "Mmmm."

"*Padawan*," I say emphatically.

"If it isn't Arden," someone sneers. "Teaching your bad lessons?" A tall, lean man stands by our table. Head tilted, he watches Coach like, like he's some wild creature. Reminds me of how Headmaster and Mr. Waters were wary of me. Convinced I was going to attack.

Behind him is the kid I fenced, OAK GROVE imprinted on his uniform.

Coach's fingers twitch. Leaning back in the booth, I can tell he's pretending calm.

"Good to see you, too, Michael. Donte, meet Jonathan Michael."

"Hello, sir."

The man isn't pleased. It's like he wants to fence verbally—*on guard*—and Coach refused. Polite, he retreated and didn't counterattack. Mr. Michael reddens. "You've forgotten your disgrace?"

(It's supposed to be a jab. Coach doesn't flinch.)

Coach waves toward me. "I was just telling Donte losing isn't disgraceful. It's how we learn."

Tension rises. Coach's words alone don't say what he's really saying. I don't understand. But Mr. Michael, fists taut, his temple vein popping, does.

Coach, though, seems almost playful. Refusing to engage, to be upset. He knows this taunts Mr. Michael but doesn't care.

If this was the schoolyard, I'd say they were getting ready to fight. Something deep, bitter is happening. I'm clueless. I can't *see.*

The kid stretches out his hand to Coach. (Manners, adults first.) "Hey, I'm Nate."

Mr. Michael—*his father?*—bats his hand away.

Nate's embarrassed. Even I want to say "I'm sorry your dad's rude."

"You don't shake hands with someone dishonorable."

Whoa. Throw down. Coach is going to blast him now.

But Coach is a statue. Chest expanding, contracting. Even, too evenly. Coach focuses on keeping himself under control. (I don't know if Mr. Michael sees it, but I do. Zarra was right—Coach runs hot. Emotional like me.)

Coach's index finger *tap-taps* the table. It's repetitive, nerve-racking. "You still think you're right about everything as ever, Michael? People make mistakes. Not everyone is defined by their mistakes. Like losing, you have to rebound. Parry and still score the touch."

Coach stands, holding himself tall, and though the two men are the same size, Coach exudes the most power. He's quiet, watchful, ready to parry. Mr. Michael wants to attack, but I can see him trying to figure out how.

"We've got to go. Nice seeing you again, Michael."

Strange. Coach's soft words seem to anger the man more.

"Dad, let's go." Nate pulls his dad's arm. His dad shrugs him off.

"There's history between us." Mr. Michael's voice grates. "Does your student know? Did you tell him about your big failure?

"I'm surprised you're teaching. You really shouldn't be teaching." Mr. Michael is baiting Coach, trying to provoke an unwise attack. Trying to score points and prove he's better. Didn't think grown-ups acted so small. Disgusting. I look at Nate. His eyes are closed like he's seen this all before. I think Mr. Michael might bully him, too.

"Coach isn't a failure," I say, empathetic, standing. "He's the best coach. Best manager at the Boys and Girls Club."

"So that's where you work." Mr. Michael laughs. "Quite a comedown."

"Good day, Michael. It's been a pleasure seeing you. I always wondered if you'd grow up; now I know." Coach never stops looking at Michael. He adds, "I see you, Michael. I didn't then. But I see you now."

Then he offers his hand to Nate. "Nice to meet you."

Nate shakes it. Scowling, his father doesn't move.

"You played well, son. Come on, Donte."

My mind is blown. I don't know all of what went down, but I know it's somehow about race. Just like the shouts "black girl," "black brother, black brother," and even my lingering fear that I might be arrested . . . all of it is about race.

Mr. Michael is a grown-up Alan.

CAR TALK

"Aren't you mad?"

Coach's car is a rusty red Ford. His hands gripping the wheel, his keychain dangles from the ignition.

"Life's too short to be mad."

"Mr. Michael seemed mad."

"Too bad for him. Jonathan Michael. Grew up believing the world was created for him."

"You feel sorry for him?" I ask, disbelieving.

Coach stares ahead, squinting. "Yes, yes, I do."

Summer sun beats down on the glass. Inside, the car warms. Outside, I see mainly parked cars. Stragglers leaving the arena: some kids and parents downcast; some, happy. I wish I could buy everyone doughnuts from the shop across the street.

"Thanks, Coach. For the doughnuts." (I burp. I should've drank more milk.)

Coach turns the key, the engine engages. I'm sad—I don't want to go home yet. As if he read my mind, Coach presses the button to lower the windows, then turns the engine off.

We sit, quiet. Comfortable.

Coach's profile is angular, sharp. Like his face could be carved on a nickel or a quarter. His neck skin sags, though. Wrinkles crisscross his arms. His hair is speckled gray and a bald spot is spreading on the back of his head.

What was he like when he was young? He's still strong, in decent shape; his moves, still fluid. Like a panther, I think. (Closing my eyes, I *see* him. Stalking with his foil, then exploding quick—lunge, attack, retreat, parry, attack.)

He must've been something. The American flag embroidered on his uniform back.

"Ask me again."

"What?"

Coach is staring, face forward. "Ask me again."

Maybe secrets should stay secret? I got what I wanted. Coach taught me fencing. But that's selfish. Coach matters, too. Zarra told me he hasn't got a family. Yet he's always helping other people's kids. Especially me. Teaching fencing, he sacrificed some of his secret. Shouldn't I know the rest?

"Why'd you stop fencing?"

"I wasn't confident enough to ignore a jerk like Michael."

"What do you mean?"

"We were on the same team. Foil. USA Fencing National Championships Team. I was the last to qualify. Beat out one of Michael's friends. He never forgave me." Coach's knuckles tighten on the wheel.

"You must've been the better fencer."

"I was. But I wasn't white. All through training, Michael harassed me."

"Didn't anybody stop him? What about your coach?"

"This was the seventies. Lots of turmoil. Civil rights activism, yes. But lots of pushback." Coach twists his body toward me. "US fencing wasn't—and still isn't—known for athletes of color.

"Michael bullied me. Called me terrible names. Threatened me. He'd convince Coach I'd broken curfew even when I hadn't. Convince teammates everything went wrong because of me."

(Like Alan, I think.)

"Worse, I buckled. Let his gaze define me. I stopped being myself, being able to see myself. Arden Jones disappeared." He sighs. "I threw a team bout."

"You lost? On purpose?" I'm shocked. Not fencing to win? I can't fathom it. It isn't fair to anyone.

"No one guessed," Coach continues, softly.

(I want to yell, "Stop.")

"Except Michael. The team didn't advance. Biggest regret of my life. Disrespecting my opponent. My team. Giving in to Michael's prejudice. For what? Pure spite."

I'm so disappointed. Tears fill my eyes. So much hurt. Coach wanted to get even. Confused, I wonder: Is Coach like me; I, like him?

Coach doesn't say anything, doesn't console me. He waits and waits.

After a while, my feelings drain, my eyes dry. I'm empty.

Sun spreads yellow, orange...red streaks across the sky. Green tree leaves flutter. Pigeons peck crumbs off the asphalt. Row after row after row, I see white parking lot lines. Most cars are gone now.

I inhale, hold my breath for three seconds, exhale.

(Why did Coach tell me his story?)

Coach never does anything without a reason. *Why now?* Why, when I'm getting ready for Middlefield try-outs? Making a play to beat Alan at his own game?

"You never played again? Michael told?"

"No, Michael didn't tell. I quit playing because I gave up on me. Became invisible."

"Why didn't Michael tell?"

"I think he knew, in a small way, he was responsible, too. His hatred caused a reaction. I'm not excusing myself. I'm responsible. Should've kept focused on my goals. Should've known bullies, biased people, can't see clearly."

"Even some adults? Teachers, police?"

"Judges, too. You've learned that, haven't you?"

I nod.

"Be you. Stay confident, visible. Even if others can't see you."

My thoughts are wild. Coach is saying some things I've felt—like how easy it'd be to give in to people's negative views. (If they think I'm a thug, why not act like one?) Like how easy it was to want revenge, to believe (no matter what) Alan's humiliation was justified.

"Why do you want to fence?" Coach barks; his voice booms inside the car.

Alan. To beat Alan. But that isn't true anymore.

"What do you dream?" The voice jars me again.

"I want to be the best." (That's the truth.)

"Time to go." He starts the car.

"Wait. Would you have told me if you hadn't seen Mr. Michael?" The car idles. Coach's hand rests on the gearshift.

"I like to think so, Donte. At first, I was afraid of letting you down, losing your respect. 'Let the past stay past.' But it's you who's given me a second chance.

"I've made my peace. Michael hasn't. He still can't see. Not me, maybe not even his own son."

"How come?"

Coach shrugs, shifts from PARK to DRIVE. "Wish I knew. Meeting you taught me to forgive myself. I don't need to hate. Not anymore."

"You love fencing." It's not a question. We gaze at each other.

"Same as you, Donte. Same as you." He twists his body toward me. "You were teaching me, too."

(Who knew?)

4

SEEING ME

MIRROR

Summertime, our garage is no longer a garage. It's a training room.

Dad placed mats over the concrete. Lined one side of the walls with mirrors. Storage boxes are now piled in the hall closet, the pantry, and Mom and Dad's bedroom closet. Mom, who always likes things neat, says, "I don't mind."

Trey, Dad, and me lift weights. Progressing to heavier and heavier dumbbells. Mirrors keep track.

Squats. Three sets of twelve. Push-ups, twenty-five. Pull-ups, ten. Mirrors show Dad, the tallest; me, the shortest. Dad, the lightest (almost pink); me, the darkest. Three bears. Trey is the middle bear. But we all are just right.

Stretch, stretch, and stretch some more. (Dad goes inside to be with Mom.)

Trey and me drill.

First position. Advance, retreat. (Do it again.) Lunge. Parry. (A hundred times.) Lunge, foil high, then lower. Right then left. Scoring on the imaginary opponent.

Mirrors reflect me. I am a fencer. I AM a fencer. Mirrors help me check my form. Mirrors show me—serious.

Cardio. An hour's run—Trey by my side.

Weekdays, we practice at the Boys and Girls Club. All day Saturday. Sundays now, too. Almost all day, every day. Training with Coach, Zion, Zarra, and Trey.

After team practice, Coach takes up a foil—and we fence. Just the two of us. Others watch, cheering. It's special seeing Coach strike like graceful lightning. Even the youngest kids sense his greatness, sense how amazing he must've been when he was young.

188

Delores, the receptionist, watches. She always claps if I score the rare touch. She likes to tease it took me forever to ask for a Boys and Girls Club membership card. The day I did, her nails were midnight blue, each with a fake diamond.

Today, her nails are lime green. She waves, wriggling her fingers.

"On guard," says Coach.

I assume first position. I already know I'm going to lose. I don't mind. (Patience.) I'm learning. Coach and his foil are teaching me infinite ways to attack, defend, deflect. Anticipate the unexpected.

Fencing someone taller, better, faster, fiercer, and more focused than me, I'm seeing ever so clear. Rising to the challenge.

I see Arden Jones, the athlete. Arden Jones sees me.

"Courage, honor, integrity, and chivalry," Coach murmurs when we finish fencing. It's a secret between us. A signal that I shouldn't make any of the mistakes he did.

Zion overhears. "Chivalry? What's chivalry?"

"Being a gentleman," I say, "earning and giving respect. Like a knight."

"Didn't knights have to be kind to women?" asks Zion.

"Everyone should be kind to everyone," snaps Zarra. Then she points her foil at her brother. "On guard. I'm kind, but I'll still beat you."

Zion rolls his eyes. He knows it's true.

Coach chuckles.

I wink. I *really, really* like Zarra. She knows it, too.

"Trey, do you want to fence?" she asks.

"Nope. You've already beaten me twice today." Trey twists his sweaty hair into a ponytail. (Zarra's the only girl who's bested him in sport.)

Zarra looks at me, winking. "Fence?"

Zarra doesn't mind if I win. She knows I respect her and won't hold back. I also know that Zarra being Zarra, it's only a matter of time before she beats me.

JULY TRYOUTS

Unbelievable. There's a huge tryout crowd. Trey made his basketball mates promise to try out. Dylan is trying out. Even the ABCs—best friends Amy, Beth, and Claire—are trying out. Beth has a crush on Trey. (She knows I know.) Trey hasn't figured it out yet.

Lots of kids are supporting Trey. But I also know they're supporting me. Everyone wants the tryouts to be fair. No black brother, white brother, just a chance for anyone to be picked.

Monsieur Durant is flustered. For the longest time he's had a small, elite team, but now everyone wants to fence. Since Trey and me started fencing, everyone wants to try, give it a shot. Alan's exclusive magic doesn't work anymore.

After basic instruction, Monsieur Durant uses Alan and his team to test tryouts. Like Alan fencing Trey, it doesn't seem right. For some, though, it works.

Brent, lanky and calm, advises Dylan. He adjusts his arms, checks his foil grip. Dylan's smiling, having fun, I think. Brent, though he's not the team's best, likes teaching. Dylan lunges, nearly tipping over. Brent steadies him.

I scan the gym. Marvin and Josh are encouraging eager kids. Dave is focused on Amy, Beth, and Claire. Flirting, swiping his foil, acting arrogant. He misses that Amy's footwork is quick, perfectly balanced. She's a natural like Zarra.

I'm supposed to be on the floor, trying out. But I hold back. Don't know why.

My body isn't trembling or jittery-crazy. I'm strangely calm. I like the view from the bleachers. Seeing excited classmates balancing foils.

Monsieur walks like a skittish peacock.

Dave is Trey's partner now. He's acting like a jerk, trying to show off, score points. But Trey's holding his own. He's not a beginner anymore.

Danny and Alan are a problem. Mean, they're embarrassing new kids. (Either Monsieur doesn't see or doesn't care to stop them.) Alan is King Selfish. Danny, his number two, a lightweight follower. The two are needling, making fun of inexperienced players. (They're not being nice.) Petey, a sixth grader, blushes red, drops his foil, and leaves the gym.

Alan and Danny high-five. (So sad.)

Headmaster McGeary steps over bleachers, heading toward me. "Great turnout," he says, stroking his blue tie.

"Yeah."

He stands two bleachers below me, making our heads and faces level. He's never apologized. (Maybe because Mom is still suing?) I look directly at him, my face blank yet confident.

"Aren't you going to try out? Monsieur Durant saw you at the preseason meet. Said you weren't bad. You'd be an asset for the team, Donte."

I blink, try not to show I'm stunned. I scan the Alan Davies Family Gymnasium. It really is beautiful. So much better than the Boys and Girls Club gym. Hanging on the wall is a huge blue banner with the crossed swords, gold lettering, and the script *Non Nobis Solum*.

"What does *non nobis solum* mean?"

" 'Not for ourselves alone.' "

"You mean like caring for one another, making a community?"

Headmaster looks at me strangely. "That's what we value at Middlefield Prep."

I almost laugh. (Now that he's heard I might be good at fencing, I'm no longer the suspicious black kid.)

I start to get angry, then relax. (Why should I care how Headmaster sees me?)

I see myself. I'm good.

Why'd I ever think I needed to beat Alan?

"Practice bout," Monsieur calls. "Everyone except Alan and Danny to the stands."

Kids spread out on the bleachers. I'm still standing on the top row with the best view.

Trey sits in the front row, his basketball crew beside and behind him.

Even a practice bout is thrilling. Alan and Danny are about to show how it's done.

With me quiet, Headmaster McGeary heads toward the floor.

Alan and Danny put on their masks, delicately yet firmly grip their swords. They salute each other, Monsieur, the audience. Some kids giggle; others applaud, though they're not supposed to. Intense, his elbows on his knees, Trey watches. Amy, I notice, is poised forward.

"En garde."

Perfect form. Wow. The two of them look amazing.

"Engage."

Like a laser beam, Danny's foil touches Alan's chest.

"Point," shouts Monsieur.

I can't see Alan's face, but I can tell he's annoyed.

He paces, foil flicking, and walks in a tight circle before settling into first position.

Danny tries the same tactic. Alan's ready for him and parries, and attacks. Danny, defending, leaves his left side vulnerable. He recovers, lunges again. Alan parries. Counter riposte. Point.

Knees bent, feet sliding smooth and fluid, Alan quickly retreats. On guard.

I *see*. Alan holds back. Fences like Brent did, seemingly passive, without energy. But, unlike Brent, he reverses course, stunning at warp speed—lunging, legs, arms, foil extending, then retreating. A blink of an eye. Danny is bewildered, caught completely off guard when he's touched. His masked head shakes.

Alan's not always in warp drive. Sometimes his attack is half-hearted, a pretense. Other times, on point.

The trick is trying to figure which attack is coming when.

There's got to be a tell. (See.) I squint, watching every move.

Danny's form weakens, falls apart. Sloppily, he attacks.

Flick, Alan deflects, then barely lunges, retreats. Danny parries, then lunges. A miss. Alan retreats, another attack, but, intentionally (it seems), not a touch. His arm, foil, retreats just before a point.

I'd be angry if Alan had the advantage, the right-of-way, and didn't fully commit to attacking. Disrespectful. *(Is it just tactics? Insulting? Or both?)*

Two minutes remain. Score: two to one.

Danny doesn't want to lose. I suspect inside he's gathering all his energy, courage, and focus. Lunge, attacking after the parry, he retreats, but not far enough; his defense fails. Three to one.

A minute more.

"Engage." First position, swords angle, make an *X*.

Alan's left arm up, hand flopped over. Normal.

"Fence."

His left fingers jerk. Warp speed. Alan lunges, his foil arcing toward Danny's chest. Incredibly, Danny parries, attacks. Alan's sword swoops, circling Danny's foil, pulling it away from the trunk and out. *Leap*, Alan lunges, the blade flexing high, the point hitting Danny's chest. Score. Four to one.

Time runs out.

Everyone claps. Alan bows. No one pays attention to Danny, mask off, face sweating, head and upper back bowed. He rubs his chest where the touch, too hard, bruised.

Alan won the mind game fair and square. Yet his win leaves a bad taste in my mouth. It's just an exhibition, not a real match. Needlessly, without mercy, he beat his friend, his team lieutenant. (Did he really have to do that now?)

Kids rush Alan. "Teach me. Show me." Monsieur beams. Alan, with his mask off, grins, searches the stands for me. His triumphant look saying *I'm better than you, better than everyone.* (Sad he humiliated Danny to send a message.)

I stare at the back of Trey's head. (Turn, I think.)

Trey turns and looks at me, his brows raised. *What?*

I jerk my head left. (He understands.) Trey gathers his gear. I step down. Row after row to the gym floor.

Not for ourselves alone. Such a joke. In different ways, Headmaster and Alan both reveal Middlefield's hypocrisy.

Boys and Girls Club. That's my fencing home. My team.

Alan has a tell. (I wish I'd seen it sooner...wish I'd see it again.) No doubt Alan is a better, more experienced fencer than me. Yet I might be able to use his own strategy against him. Poke his ego. Exploit his flaws.

Be tougher inside my mind.

BOOK SENSE

Stretching before practice. Trey's hamstrings are tight. Zion, legs outstretched, twists and bends his back. I stretch my feet, calves, quads, abs, arms, neck, everything. Need to get ready.

I've never felt so comfortable in my body. I've stopped twitching, feeling roiling anger in my gut, and my arms, legs always do what I tell them.

On the wood bleacher, Coach is reading papers, filling out forms for fencing meets. He's got an office the size of a closet. He never uses it. He likes to keep close to his team.

(I get it.) Spread across the gym floor, I feel among family. Only Zarra is missing.

The gym door opens. Zarra hollers, "What's up?" She drags a heavy tote bag.

Trey reaches out, pushes me. He knows I'm happier when Zarra's here.

"What you got?" calls Zion.

"Books."

"You've been to the library?" asks Trey.

"You know it." Zarra plops down, emptying the tote on the floor.

"Any science fiction?" I ask.

"Nonfiction, it's better."

Zion, Trey, and me reach, grabbing for the books.

Olympic Fencing has a Post-it note sticking out.

"Open it," says Zarra, scooting beside Zion, reading, "Erinn Smart. African American woman foil fencer. Won team silver in the 2008 Beijing Summer Olympics."

"Coach, you told her to look it up," pipes Zion, proud of his big sister.

"So I did." Coach joins us, sitting on the floor like us kids.

"There's lots of women fencers," exclaims Zarra. "I thought they'd all be white. Mostly, but not all. There's Ibtihaj Muhammad. She's Muslim American and fences in a hijab."

"She won team bronze in the 2016 Rio Olympics," adds Coach.

"Ibtihaj trained with Peter Westbrook. So did Erinn Smart. Here's his book." Zarra slides over *Harnessing Anger: The Inner Discipline of Athletic Excellence.*

The book's title alone makes me think I'd understand Mr. Westbrook. He'd understand me. I glance at Coach. His expression's grim.

"Westbrook's a six-time Olympian," pipes Zarra. "He's got a foundation in New York. Trains thousands of inner-city kids."

"You mean I didn't have to come to Boston to fence?" I joke.

Coach smiles slightly.

"And..." Zarra pauses dramatically, "...the 2016 Olympic team had five..." Another pause. "FIVE"— she holds up her hand, spreading her five fingers—

"fencers of color." Gleeful, Zarra reaches into her tote and pulls out a magazine. "The librarian let me borrow her copy." She flips to another Post-it note.

"Wow, oh, wow." I'm stunned. All of us are thrilled. We lean closer.

Five—*FIVE*—faces of color. Two girls. Three guys. Ibtihaj Muhammad, Nzingha Prescod, and Daryl Homer all trained with Westbrook. Jason Pryor is from Ohio. Miles Chamley-Watson is biracial *AND* British and American.

"Amazing." Trey's fingers lightly touch the photos. "This could be any one of you."

"Or you, Trey," I say.

"I told you," Coach murmurs, "all of you belong in fencing."

"Why around here are fencers mainly white?" asks Trey.

"Racial bias. But class bias, too. Public schools don't offer fencing. Private schools do."

"Like lacrosse. Trey and me never knew the sport existed until we started private school."

"Yeah, like water polo, too." Trey nods.

"Segregated pools kept generations of inner-city

kids from swimming," adds Coach. "I still don't know how to swim."

Nobody says anything.

Then Zion whispers, "Zarra and me can't swim."

"Trey and me can't, either. Not many pools in the city."

"Ball sports are cheaper," mutters Trey. "I go to private school now, but I grew up playing ball."

We're all quiet again. Even Coach.

"It's not fair," Zarra complains. "Everyone should have a chance to play sports. All kinds of sports. Money and skin color shouldn't matter.

"You know what else isn't fair?" Zarra taps the cover of *The Three Musketeers*. "Alexandre Dumas."

"Who?" I blurt.

"One of the most famous authors ever."

Trey elbows me. "Donte, don't you remember 'All for one, and one for all'?"

"That's him? This Dumas guy?"

"Not *mas* but *ah*—Du-*mah*. A black Frenchman."

"Whoa," I explode. "In movies, on TV, musketeers are always white."

"I know. But Dumas was writing about his dad!"

Zarra slides over another book—*The Black Count* by Tom Reiss. "Dumas's dad was the greatest general in Napoleon's army."

We all stare. A black man on a horse, wearing a military uniform—white pants, white gloves, navy jacket, and a blue, white, and red sash. His hat is black, pointed on two sides, his sword with a gold hilt is raised high. But it's his face that's amazing. Strong, fiercely calm, solid.

Zarra sighs. "Isn't he something? In *The Three Musketeers*, the scene where D'Artagnan fights all the three musketeers at once is based on Dumas's dad. For real. And look, the subtitle: *Glory, Revolution, Betrayal, and the Real Count of Monte Cristo.*"

"What's that mean?" asks Trey.

Coach speaks, soft. "*The Count of Monte Cristo.* Another great Dumas book. An innocent man is betrayed, accused of treason, imprisoned, and after many long years, escapes. Napoleon, jealous of General Dumas, sent him to jail."

My back straightens.

"A powerful white man," Coach says, woeful, "jailed an innocent black man. Dumas was disappeared."

I exhale. "If people didn't see him, he didn't exist." (Shuddering, I remember how close I came to being disappeared.)

"General Thomas-Alexandre Dumas was forgotten," answers Coach. "Born in 1762, a son of a slave. For a short time, a slave himself."

"You've read the book, Coach?"

Coach nods. "Yes, Zarra, many times. Dumas's life was the real adventure story."

"Yes! From Haiti, he sailed to Paris. His father was a marquess. That's just below a duke," she adds, turning toward Zion.

"The marquess made sure Dumas could fence. Skilled, courageous, Dumas was famous right up to the day he was jailed."

"Wow. That could be a movie." I touch the jacket cover, General Dumas's face.

"There're movies. *The Three Musketeers. Man in the Iron Mask. The Count of Monte Cristo*, and more. Hollywood controls the story. Black fencers like Dumas were erased."

(How many years? I quickly calculate. About 258 years.)

"Mr. Westbrook is trying to change that?" Zion's voice squeaks.

"He *is* changing it," Zarra says, emphatic. "We should start a foundation. The Arden Jones Foundation."

"No," Coach snaps irritably, surprising Zarra, Zion, and Trey. "Mr. Westbrook has the true legacy."

There's a trust between us. Coach never asked me to keep his secret—how anger derailed his career.

(I get it. Finally get it. Coach teaches me to do better. *Be better.* Seeing myself outscores hate.)

"Coach, you're the best," I say, heartfelt.

"Donte, Trey, Zion, and Zarra." He gazes at each of us. "You're my legacy. A coach's dream." He stands, gruffly shouting, "Grab your foils."

Serious, we leap up, erect, tall—our foils at our sides.

Coach grins, points his sword high. "'All for one, one for all.'"

Each of us lifts steel swords, touching, crossing each other, pointing skyward. "'All for one, one for all.'"

(We've already won.)

SUCCESS

Fencing is physical—balancing form,
distance, and precise moves.

Fencing is mental—balancing respect for
the sport, self-confidence, and calm.

Greatness blends mind and body—not
by winning against an opponent, but by
focusing on your mind guiding the blade.

Fencing is life. The battle is always
centered in the self.

—Rising to the Fencing Challenge

THIS IS ME. DONTE

HEAD HIGH

Coach believes in me. I believe in me.

Teammates, we believe in each other.

We stride into the arena. Not many fencers of color in the Massachusetts regional. But we feel Dumas and his father, the Black Count, and all the fencers of the Peter Westbrook Foundation (though we've never met any!) striding with us.

We belong here.

We're waiting to march around the arena. I look across at Trey. He's gotten taller, more flexible. He's a good fencer. But I'm better. (Who'd have thought?) This is my first sport, the first time we've done a sport together.

Mom and Dad are in the stands. Mom shouts our names; Dad whistles. (They're embarrassing. But it's good.) Next to Mom, Zion and Zarra's mom waves a Jamaican flag.

"I can't believe she took a day off," coos Zarra, shaking my arm. "Mom always says, 'No work, no food.'"

"She's proud of you. Me too."

The loudspeaker rumbles: "Greater Boston Boys and Girls Club."

Our team walks solid, bold. No bowed heads, just joy. Coach, serious, struts beside us—erect, glowing, looking like the Olympian he once was.

This regional competition is the real deal. Bouts are three periods of three minutes each with a minute rest between each period. To advance from qualifying rounds to quarterfinals, semifinals to the finals, you have to win each bout. Win.

Middlefield Prep sits a couple of teams down from us. Trey waves at Brent. Coach and Monsieur Durant nod. (Battle lines are drawn.)

I keep calm. (Or at least try to.) I can feel my old worries, insecurities circling inside me. Funny how I know I don't have to prove anything....I still feel like I have to prove something. That I'm not "less than." (I know.) Still, Alan's racism is like an echo in my bones, mind, and blood. Another unfairness. I'm the one wasting energy, suppressing memories, words.

(Focus, Donte. Focus.)

I inhale, count to three, exhale. My foot starts trembling. Bouncing. I inhale, count to three again. Exhale.

On the bench, Zarra sits next to me. "We've got this."

I feel better. I see Alan being Alan. Farther down the row, he's standing, circled by his teammates. Giving a pep talk, I think. Showing his swagger, dominating everyone.

Some of the Middlefield newbies sit quietly on the

bench. I wave. Dylan waves back. (I'm glad he made the team.) Amy did, too.

A buzzer sounds. Bouts begin.

Zarra steps onto the field. Across from her, a brunette. Both put their masks on. You can't tell who's who. Who's white. Who's black. Just two fencers trying to score.

Zarra is on point. She reminds me of a cat. A bobcat—yeah. Fierce, compact, roaming desert, forest, urban edges. Adaptable, intent. Fluid until she strikes. She's going to win. Her body weight is centered in first position, her legs and feet shift, slide, independent of her trunk. Then, crazy, her whole body, legs, arms, hands, and feet strike, unified.

Score. A touch.

I want to cheer, leap into the air. Coach excitedly rubs his hands together. Zion murmurs, "That's my sister. She killed it."

I glance at Trey. He's scowling, ripping, balling paper with his fist.

Zarra keeps scoring like a musketeer.

Stooping before Trey, I whisper, "What's the matter?"

He shakes his head.

But I know my big brother. His face flushes red, and, I swear, his eyes are too bright. (Tears? My big brother?)

Trey brushes his eyes, brow. "I'm okay."

My hand clasps his—black over white. With my other hand, I peel back his fingers. Trey resists. Then, ultimately, relaxes.

Two pieces of paper. I unfurl one. *Why play with...* I don't open the second. I don't want to see a hateful word.

Coach steps across, bending down. "Problem?"

"No, Coach. Someone's nasty, stupid note." Trey opens his palm. Torn paper falls.

"You lose with your mind." Reminding me of Dad, Coach grips Trey's shoulder. Squeezes. "You're okay." A statement.

Trey stuffs the note in his pocket. "Yeah, I'm cool."

In the stands, Mom and Dad watch us. Mom's brow is furrowed. Her emotions fresh on her face. I smile, do a thumbs-up. Look at Dad. (He knows. Something bad happened.)

He holds up his hand, high-fiving the air.

I hold my hand up, too. (Dad knows us Ellison brothers can handle it.)

Zarra wins her match and advances. Zion does, too.

Trey loses in the first round. But he fenced well. His opponent was just tough.

I advance to the next round and the next.

Zarra and I both breeze through to the semifinals.

For the semi-pairing, I'm fencing Nate Michael. He's beaten me before, but that matters less than knowing he's a good, fair opponent.

We're wired for electric scoring. Masks cover our faces. Warm breath swirls inside the mesh. Air seems rare, needing to be saved for a burst. Steel mesh alters my sight. Every part of my body covered, my hands gloved, I feel transformed.

The foil feels natural. Like it was made for my hand.

Nate and I salute.

The semifinal is a five-touch bout.

"On guard."

We assume our stance. First position.

"Ready?"

(I'm ready.)

"Fence."

I'm in the zone. Fencing is warp speed but my mind slows time. Watching how the blade moves, I can *see* before it arrives. I parry. Counterattack.

Nate's reach is amazing. But I'm quicker. I retreat, keeping distance close enough to escape attack. Close enough to attack.

Parry and riposte. First touch!

We start again.

"On guard." (First position.)

"Ready?" (Yeah. I'm ready.)

"Fence."

Lunge, a quick, almost flying attack. Nate surprises me, touches my left side. (I missed it.) Stupid.

First position. Exhale. I flick my fingers, my blade slightly.

"Ready? Fence."

I see everything. My breath evens out. My heartbeat calms. Nothing exists beyond light, flexible blades.

Parry, riposte. Touch. Point for me.

Nate's off-balance.

A thousand different ways to attack. I'm ready for any of them. Parry. Parry. Riposte. Parry, riposte.

Nate's frustrated, erratic. His blade quivers. The more emotion he feels, the less I do.

Another period. Another three minutes. Might as well be triple the time. Nate doesn't have a strategy. He's flailing. I don't get it.

(Maybe he's surprised by how much better I've gotten? Maybe he's flustered because he expected to win?)

My strategy is to take advantage of his mistakes. Wait for his attack, respond like a flash. When he rushes too wild. When he retreats too slow. Touch. He keeps being hit—point after point after point. I win five to one! No need for a third period.

Walking back to my team, I focus on my teammates' delight. Trey's smile. Zarra doing a happy dance. Zion hooting and hollering, "Get down." (Or something like that.) Coach is over the moon, pumping his fists like a champ.

Crossing in front of the Middlefield Prep team, Alan trips me. My mask rolls forward. I drop my foil, trying to break my fall. A painful shock sears my wrist. I recover, cradling my hand.

"Clumsy brother?" Alan thinks it's all a joke. Monsieur Durant, clueless, doesn't see. Danny, Alan's lieutenant, picks up my foil. I'm surprised. Dylan scurries after my mask.

"Thanks, guys." I say, surprised.

Snap, snap. Coach activates two cold packs. A towel on my lap, he lays the packs on my right hand and wrist.

"Advil?"

"Sure, Donte."

None of us—Trey, Zion, Zarra, or Coach—admit I

was tripped on purpose. I avoid looking in the stands for Mom and Dad.

My wrist hurts.

"You did fine, Donte." Zarra's eyes are so sad. (Makes me want to hug her.)

"Agreed," says Coach. "You gave your best."

Then it hits me. They're expecting me to quit.

(Should I quit?)

I look about the arena. There's no other Boys and Girls Club team. No other team that looks like ours.

Teasing, my brother, sitting behind me, puts me in a mock choke hold. "Hey," he says into my ear, "you've got game."

I try to see his face. Trey's grip is rigid. I can only see what's in front of me.

The last semifinal match—Country Day School v. Middlefield Prep. George Hansen v. Alan Davies.

The opponents salute.

I breathe heavily, nervously. I'm supposed to fence whoever wins.

"Feel me," Trey says, confident. His words calm me like rippling water.

"I feel you."

"You're my best brother."

"Your only brother."

Chuckling, Trey's breath tickles my ear. "Close your eyes, Donte. Remember: Together, forever. I'm your black brother."

"I'm your white brother."

I open my eyes.

Alan scores.

Zion and Zarra scoot sideways, making it easy for Trey to squeeze in, sit beside me. For a few seconds, the people, the bout fall away. Despite our physical differences, it's like looking into a mirror.

(Another touch. Another, and another. Alan is indomitable.)

Trey's as black as me; I'm as white as him. We're both our parents' sons. Mixed-bloods.

My gaze flicks about the arena. Everybody else is mixed-blood, too.

"I'm not quitting," I say.

Trey stands, daring Coach to contradict.

Coach's lips curve upward. "Skill makes the man."

Of course I'm destined to meet Alan.

Some battles can't be postponed, delayed. Avoided.

In the finals, Alan will be my opponent. One of us will be first; the other, second.

Head between my knees, I inhale, exhale. (My wrist doesn't hurt, I lie to myself.) Alan doesn't bother me.

I think of Dumas and his dad, the Black Count. (How cool is that?) Think, too, of Viking ancestors who sailed the great seas. And Mom's ancestors, who encouraged her resilience, battles for justice.

I'm not one. I'm many.

Fencing is in my blood.

Walking to the strip to meet Alan, I am more me than I've ever been.

My glove is tight on my foil hand. Alan smirks. Except for logos, our white uniforms match. We both lower our masks.

Salute. Salute. Salute.

"On guard."

Attack. It's clear Alan thinks he'll beat me. Heedless, reckless, he lunges again and again. I parry, counter-attack. Again, and again. My ripostes aren't too fast for Alan. He parries each one.

No score for anyone.

Pain swells when I'm still. In motion, I don't feel anything. Just flow.

Period One: zero to zero. (Stalemate.)

Alan is upset. I can't see his face, but he paces in a circle like he did when fencing Danny. He's frustrated. Probably thought he'd score every point against me.

I watch his left hand, his wrist in back, in line

with his head. He's trying to taunt, trick me with his relaxed, almost sloppy parrying.

Instead of being tempted, I pull back. I'm being cautious. (Really, I'm setting a trap.)

Alan's left fingers twitch.

I steady myself and he roars toward me, blade flashing, flexing, coming in for the hit. I slide back, angle my torso, and the foil tip slips right by me. Parry, counterattack. Touch.

"Touché," shouts the referee.

Alan is furious.

I can see, smell it. Dusty sweat. His trunk slightly rocking rather than still.

My wrist throbs. Cotton restricts my fingers. Knuckles ache. It's harder to balance, point, and target the foil.

"Ready? Fence."

Alan rushes, flies warp speed, coming at me again. Again. Again. My mind shouts *Retreat, retreat, retreat.* I'm getting close to the strip's end. Danger, going out of bounds.

I center myself. Stare at the foil's tip. Nothing else.
(Got to, got to, got to make the defensive move.)

Parry, frontal attack, reach high, risking my chest.
My foil bends over the top of Alan's sword and touches!

Alan roars. Two can warp speed.

I fence defensively for the rest of the period. Hold
on, I think. Just hold on.

Period Two: Two to zero.

A minute's rest.

(Coach is quiet; his eyes say, *Do you, Donte. Do you.*)
(Almost like Rocky Balboa told Adonis Creed.)

Period Three
Tired. We both hang back. Foils *tap-tapping* one another.
Not long, seconds only. But fencers always fence, and
one of us has to make a move. Me? Alan?

Has Alan learned his lesson? I study his body. His
back hand is relaxed. He's regrouped.

Danger. I'm facing King Alan. Champ.

I feint, then lunge.

Alan parries, counterattacks. I try to parry. Not good enough. Score. Point Alan.

I feel my wrist stiffening.

Fencing is a mental game.

"Ready?"

"Wait." I massage my wrist. Stopping makes Alan think I'm weak, in too much pain. But I'm restoring circulation, range of motion.

(Do the unexpected.) Get Alan feeling overconfident again.

I resume on guard position. I hold my foil lower than usual.

"Ready? Fence."

Alan beats my blade, hard.

I retreat, letting my tip waver.

He tries to beat my blade again, advancing quickly, but I slip my blade beneath his and score an easy touch.

"Touché."

I step back to my mark for the next point.

Alan, furious, beats my blade ferociously.

The crowd gasps. No on guard position. No "Ready? Fence."

"Unsportsmanlike behavior." The referee hands Alan a red card.

Alan's penalty: a point goes to me. He lines up on his mark, seething.

A minute left. I just have to hang on.

Alan's attacks are relentless; I parry, retreat.

Our blades scrape and clang. I breathe heavily, inside my mask. Parry, retreat.

With each attack, images flash: police, handcuffs, jail, courthouse, and judge.

Time ticks away. The clock is my ally. I'm up: four to one.

Almost there. I am a blur of parries. Alan can't break through.

Thirty seconds left.

Big finish. I grunt, the dam bursts, all my hurt and anger rushes through my body then narrows into a fluid, focused hit. Score.

Five to one, I win!

TRIUMPH

Pain, exhaustion overwhelm me. Then I hear applause, cheering. Hear Dad whistling from the stands. Trey shouting, "Way to go."

Zion and Zarra are jumping up and down. Coach claps, stomping his feet.

It sinks in: I've won. I feel like I can fly.

Walking toward Alan, I tug my gloves off. Extend my left, unswollen hand.

Alan won't look at me. His face is flushed, his black hair damp and slick. He reminds me of those living statues—they're thinking, feeling, sensing, but, nonetheless, seem like stone.

My hand remains outstretched.

Slowly, Alan removes his glove. He shakes my hand—his right hand to my good left.

Funny, seeing our palms and fingers entwined, I could be clasping Dad's or Trey's hand. Black on white. White on black.

Alan tries to pull his hand back. I grip harder. (Look at me.)

Alan's head lifts. "Congratulations."

I barely hear him. It doesn't matter. I know—*Alan sees me.* Next time he might win the bout. Or I might. I don't care.

He can even dislike me if he wants. But now he has to see ME.

I know who I am—Donte Ellison, son of William and Denise Ellison, brother of Trey Ellison.

Arden Jones's student; Zion and Zarra's teammate.

Me.

Everyone in the arena sees me.

Fencing champion.

I raise my foil with unshakable, unmistakable confidence.

EPILOGUE

I won gold. Zarra, silver.

We celebrated at the Boys and Girls Club. Delores cooked: ribs, black-eyed peas, and greens. Enough for an army.

"Next celebration," Zarra's mom promised, "I'll cook."

"Celebration after that, we'll order pizza." Dad and Mom, like kids, held, swung their hands.

Coach raised a plastic cup of Coke. "Let's salute our Boys and Girls Club family."

Jamil and dozens of others laughed, sang, and danced.

I introduced Zarra to Mom. They played hopscotch. Neither would tell me what they dreamed. Though I think Zarra's goal might be the Olympics. (Like mine.)

Afterward, Zion, Trey, and me hopscotched, too. Coach and Dad cheered us on.

It was a great night.

(Coach, teammates, supportive parents, and friends. Food.

How cool is that?)

———

Middlefield Prep celebrated Trey and me, too. It was nice. Accepting. Felt a little bit like a new community.

Alan wanted to quit the fencing team. But his parents wouldn't let him. Danny became team captain.

Mom's court case is ongoing. On the anniversary of me being arrested, Trey and me wore T-shirts to school.

Tuesday, my black T-shirt read in white letters: **BLACK BROTHER**. Trey's white T-shirt read in black letters: **WHITE BROTHER**.

Wednesday, my white T-shirt read in black letters:

WHITE BROTHER. Trey's black T-shirt read in white letters: **BLACK BROTHER**.

All our classmates, confused, shook their heads.

Thursday, Trey and I both wore black T-shirts with white letters: **BLACK BROTHER**.
Friday, I wore a white T-shirt with black letters: **RACE IS NOT A COLOR**. Trey wore a black T-shirt with white letters: **HERITAGE IS LIT. WHAT'S YOURS?**

Monday, the student council sponsored a Heritage Sit-in. In the gym, a table was filled with hundreds of multicolored T-shirts, felt pens, ribbons, and sparkles. We celebrated all afternoon our heritage, our mixed blood, ourselves.

One small step.

(Donte out.)

AFTERWORD

While researching *Ghost Boys*, I learned elementary through high school students of color are often unfairly suspended, arrested by police, and in many cases charged with crimes. Once arrested even for minor infractions, the odds that a student will be entrapped by the criminal justice system and not graduate double (https://www.tolerance.org/magazine/spring-2013 /the-school-to-prison-pipeline).

Some cases against children of color are mind-boggling—e.g., a middle school student who normally gets a milk carton with his free lunch was handcuffed and accused of larceny; a seven-year-old, crying because of bullying, was handcuffed and arrested for not complying with commands to stop making noise. Undoubtedly, both students suffered mental and emotional trauma.

In *Black Brother, Black Brother*, I felt compelled to explore both racism and colorism affecting two biracial brothers. Classmates, knowing two brothers are genetically related prefer the lighter of the two. This prejudice is reinforced by Hollywood, media, and historic cultural biases that privilege white skin, and even lighter skin within the same ethnic group, over black skin tones. Yet black/white categories are a falsehood.

Artist Angélica Dass in her Humanae Project (https://www.angelicadass.com/humanae-project/) has classified over four thousand skin tones among humans and demonstrates how impossible it is to reduce humanity to binary opposites—i.e., black and white.

My grandmother taught me that everyone is a "mixed-blood stew" and that diversity of appearance (skin color, hair, and eye color) are to be celebrated. Everyone is human and everyone carries an ethnic heritage that results from the origins and journeys their ancestors made.

My two biracial children (one, light-skinned; the

other, darker) have had very different experiences growing up in America. Skin color should not determine the ease with which one child is more fully embraced by society and the other is subject to racism. Like Donte and Trey in *Black Brother, Black Brother*, they should be treated equally and one not privileged over the other because of skin color.

Ending racism sometimes seems like a never-ending battle. But I believe it is a battle that can be won. Progress has been made and I believe that the world's youth are going to make bolder and greater strides toward equity. Poems, raps, stories, and essays that students have sent remind me that young people are "bearing witness" and advocating for social justice.

Now, why fencing? Over thirty-five years ago, I discovered in a *Smithsonian* magazine article that the French author Alexandre Dumas had African heritage. For decades, Hollywood colorism represented Dumas's characters as white, ensuring for generations that many Americans would read and imagine fencing as a white-only sport. (In 2019, the United Kingdom production company Neon Ink began working on a television adaptation of *The Count of Monte Cristo* with the Count played by a black actor.) Later, reading *The Black Count: Glory, Revolution, Betrayal, and the Real Count of Monte Cristo* by Tom Reiss, I learned that Dumas's father was the son of a black slave and a French aristocrat. Alex Dumas, the father, became a famous general in Napoleon's army and was the model for most of his son's heroes.

How many children of color failed to dream of becoming a fencer because of a white master literary and media narrative?

Amazingly, the 2016 US Olympic fencing team comprised several African American fencers (https://www.ebony.com/entertainment/olympics-rio-black-fencers/) as well as multiple Asian American fencers (https://asamnews.com/2016/08/04/asian-americans-go-to-rio-olympics-to-make-a-point/).

Ben Bratton, a three-time fencing all-American, and the first African American and youngest to win a gold medal at the World Team Championships, introduced me to the Peter Westbrook Foundation, which has trained numerous inner-city youth that have gone on to excel in college, national, and international fencing competitions.

Ben, an épée fencer, teaches at the Peter Westbrook Foundation. Watching him and his recent Olympian colleagues teach a hundred young boys and girls of color on a Saturday morning in New York was thrilling.

Alexandre Dumas would have, I believe, honored Peter Westbrook for his accomplishments. I highly recommend reading Peter Westbrook's memoir (written with Tej Hazarika), *Harnessing Anger: The Inner Discipline of Athletic Excellence*.

DISCUSSION QUESTIONS

1. Donte and Trey have a strong brotherly bond. How do they make space for each other? How do they include each other?

2. How do Donte and Trey's friends support them? What specific actions do they take to make Donte and Trey feel safer and more included at school? What do you think it means to be an ally?

3. How do people react to Trey and his dad compared to Donte and his mom?

4. Fencing is described as an elite sport. What barriers make fencing difficult for more people to get involved in?

5. Coach eventually reveals his personal history with fencing to Donte. How do these revelations about Coach's past affect Donte's decisions in the

present? How does Donte benefit from having Coach as a role model?

6. How does Donte change as he learns to fence? In what ways does he begin to think differently?

7. Donte remarks that he's "got to be careful" walking around his neighborhood (p. 33). Why does Donte think this? How does this awareness affect his interactions with authority figures like his headmaster and the police?

8. The Middlefield Prep school motto is *non nobis solum*, which the headmaster translates as "not for ourselves alone" (p. 194). Do you think Middlefield lives up to this motto? How so?

9. Zarra tells Donte about the Alexandre Dumas biography *The Black Count*. How do the stories we are told impact how we view the world? Does history always show us the full story?

10. Through training, Donte discovers that fencing is a sport based on rules and etiquette. How can you apply the rules of fencing, namely "courage, honor, integrity, and chivalry," to your everyday life (p. 189)?

ACKNOWLEDGMENTS

Writing a book requires a team. My team is among the best!

Thank you to Alvina Ling, my brilliant editor, and Ruqayyah Daud, her talented editorial assistant. Michael Bourret, my agent, who supports me always.

A special thank you and hug to my husband, Brad, who is my literary and life soulmate.

ACKNOWLEDGMENTS

Turn the page for a sneak preview of

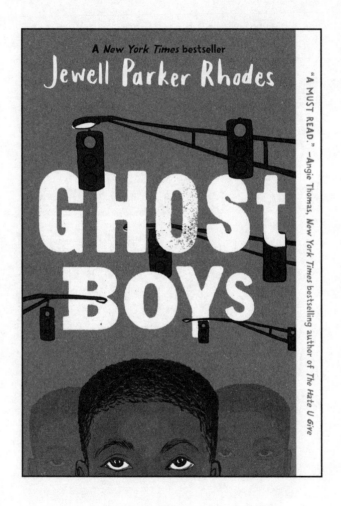

AVAILABLE NOW

DEAD

How small I look. Laid out flat, my stomach touching ground. My right knee bent and my brand-new Nikes stained with blood.

I stoop and stare at my face, my right cheek flattened on concrete. My eyes are wide open. My mouth, too.

I'm dead.

I thought I was bigger. Tough. But I'm just a bit of nothing.

My arms are outstretched like I was trying to fly like Superman.

I'd barely turned, sprinting. *Pow, pow.* Two bullets. Legs gave way. I fell flat. Hard.

I hit snowy ground.

Ma's running. She's wailing, "My boy. My boy." A policeman holds her back. Another policeman is standing over me, murmuring, "It's a kid. It's a kid."

Ma's struggling. She gasps like she can't breathe; she falls to her knees and screams.

I can't bear the sound.

Sirens wail. Other cops are coming. Did someone call an ambulance?

I'm still dead. Alone on the field. The policeman closest to me is rubbing his head. In his hand, his gun dangles. The other policeman is watching Ma like she's going to hurt someone. Then, he shouts, "Stay back!"

People are edging closer, snapping pictures, taking video with their phones. "Stay back!" The policeman's hand covers his holster.

More people come. Some shout. I hear my name. "Jerome. It's Jerome." Still, everyone stays back. Some curse; some cry.

Doesn't seem fair. Nobody ever paid me any attention. I skated by. Kept my head low.

Now I'm famous.

Chicago Tribune
OFFICER: "I HAD NO CHOICE!"

Jerome Rogers, 12, shot at abandoned Green Street lot. Officer says, "He had a gun."

ALIVE

December 8
Morning

"Come straight home. You hear me, Jerome? Come straight home."

"I will." I always do.

Ma leans down, hugs me. Grandma slides another stack of pancakes on my plate. "Promise?"

"Promise." Same ritual every day.

I stuff a pancake into my mouth. Kim sticks out her tongue.

I'm the good kid. Wish I wasn't. I've got troubles but I don't get *in* trouble. Big difference.

I'm pudgy, easily teased. But when I'm a grown-up, everybody's going to be my friend. I might even be president. Like Obama.

Kim says she believes me. That's why I put up with her.

She can be annoying. Asking too many questions.

Like: "What makes a cloud?" "Why're their shapes different?" Telling me: "*Minecraft* is stupid." Begging me to help pick out a library book.

"Hurry up. Else you'll be late," says Grandma. She hands Ma a lunch sack. At school, me and Kim get free lunch.

Everybody works in our house. Ma is a receptionist at Holiday Inn. Her shift starts at eight a.m.

Me and Kim's job, says Ma, is going to school.

Pop leaves the house at four a.m. He's a sanitation officer. He drives a truck. In the old days, there was a driver and two men hanging off the truck's sides, leaping down to lift and dump smelly trash cans. Now steel arms pick up bins. Pop does the whole route by himself. He stays in the air-conditioned cabin, steering, pressing the button for the mechanical arm, and listening to Motown. The Temptations. Smokey Robinson. The Supremes. Sixties pop music. Lame. Hip-hop is better.

Grandma keeps house. She cooks, cleans. Makes it so me and Kim aren't home alone. Have snacks. Homework help (though I prefer playing video games).

"After school is troublesome," says Ma.

Pushing back my chair, I kiss her.

"Come straight home," Ma repeats, tucking in her white uniform shirt.

Grandma hugs, squeezes me like I'm a balloon. She pecks my cheek. "I'm worried about you. Been having bad dreams."

"Don't worry." That's my other job—comforting Ma and Grandma. Grandma worries the most. She has dreams. "Premonitions," she calls them. Worries about bad things happening. But I don't know what, where, when, or why.

"Sometimes I dream lightning strikes. Or earthquakes. Sometimes it's dark clouds mushrooming in the sky. I wake troubled."

Remembering her words, I worry. I know Ma will remind her to take her blood pressure pill.

Pop worries, too, but he usually doesn't say so. Early morning, before he leaves for work, he always stops by my room. (Kim's, too.)

He opens the door; there's a shaft of hallway light. I've gotten used to it. Eyes closed, I pretend to be asleep. Pop looks and looks, then softly closes the door and goes to work.

"Jerome?" Grandma clasps my shoulder. "Tell me three good things."

I pause. Grandma is truly upset. Half-moon shadows rim her eyes.

"Three, Jerome. Please."

Three. Grandma's special number. "Three means 'All.' Optimism. Joy," Grandma says every day. "Heaven, Earth, Water. Three means you're close to the angels."

I lick my lip. "One, school is fun." Hold up two fingers. "I like it when it snows." Then, "Three, when I'm grown, I'm going to have a cat." (A dog, too. But I don't say that. A dog would be *four* good things. Can't ruin the magical three.)

Grandma exhales. I've said exactly what she needed to hear. *Fine,* I've told her. *I'm fine.*

I stuff my books into my bag. I wink, wave bye to Ma.

"Study hard," she says, both smiling and frowning.

She's happy I comforted Grandma, but unhappy with Grandma's southern ways.

Ma wants me and Kim to be "ED—YOU—CATED." She pokes her finger at us when she says "YOU."

"ED—YOU"—*poke*—"CATED, Jerome." Sometimes the poke hurts a bit. But I get it.

Grandma dropped out of elementary school to care for her younger sisters. Ma and Pop finished high school. Me and Kim are supposed to go to college.

Kim is by the front door, backpack slung over her shoulder. Kim's nice. But I don't tell her that. She's bony, all elbows and knees. When she's a teenager, I'll be grown. Everybody will worry more about her than me.

Ma always says, "In this neighborhood, getting a child to adulthood is perilous."

I looked up the word. *Perilous.* "Risky, dangerous."

I pull Kim's braid. Frowning, she swats my hand.

Can't be good all the time.

Later, I'll take my allowance and buy Kim a book. Something scary, fun.

We walk to school. Not too fast like we're running; not too slow like we're daring someone to stop us. Our walk has got to be just right.

Green Street isn't peaceful; it isn't green either. Just brick houses, some lived in, some abandoned. Out-of-work men play cards on the street, drinking beer from cans tucked in paper bags.

Eight blocks to travel between home and school.

On the fifth block from our house is Green Acres. A meth lab exploded there and two houses burnt. Neighbors tried to clear the debris, make a basketball court. It's pathetic. A hoop without a net. Spray-painted lines. Planks of wood hammered into sad bleachers. At least somebody tried.

Two blocks from school, drug dealers slip powder or pill packets to customers, stuffing cash into their pockets. Pop says, "Not enough jobs, but still, it's wrong. Drugs kill." Me and Kim cross the street, away from the dealers. They're not the worst, though. School bullies are the worst. Bullies never leave you alone. Most days I try to stay near adults. Lunchtime I hide in the locker room, the supply closet, or the bathroom.

Kim slips her hand in mine. She knows.

"I'll meet you after school," I say.

"You always do." She squeezes my palm. "You going to have a good day?"

"Yeah," I say, trying to smile, searching the sidewalks for Eddie, Snap, and Mike. They like to dump my backpack. Push me, pull my pants down. Hit me upside the head.

Kim clenches her hand, purses her lips. She's smart for a third grader. She knows surviving the school day isn't easy for me.

She never tells.

Ma, Pop, and Grandma have enough to worry about. They know Kim's popular and I'm not. But they don't need to know I'm being bullied.

"Kimmeee!" a girl shouts.

Kim flashes me a grin. I nod. Then she skips up

the school steps, her braids bouncing as she and Keisha chatter-giggle, crossing left into the elementary school. Middle school is to the right.

"Yo, Jerome."

I look over my shoulder, hugging my backpack closer. Mike's grinning. Eddie and Snap, fists clenched, thug-posing, stand by his side. Damn. Have to be super careful.

During lunch, I'll hide in the bathroom. Maybe they'll forget about me? Find another target?

I can hope.

Just like I hope I'll win the lottery. A million dollars.